The Mystery of the

Hidden Cabin

M E Hembroff

Dedication

I dedicate this book to my family and friends

THANK YOU

I would like to thank all the people who have helped in the production of this book even if in a small way. I thank Claudia Elliot for reading a rough copy and making helpful recommendations. Also, Susan Utlendorfsky for her helpful editing suggestions. Last but not least I want to thank Claire Plaisted and her team for the final stages of producing my book.

Contents

Chapter 1 New School

Aunt Anna, Megan's mother, dropped us off on her way to work at the general store. Megan, my cousin, and I walked down the crumbly sidewalk where grass and wild flowers flourished between the cracks, toward Pineview School. My mind wandered as I ran my fingers over the feathery grass near the edge. It was my first day at a new school, and I was nervous and excited at the same time. I wasn't sure what to wear but finally decided on my red skirt with a white poodle on one side and a white blouse. It hadn't left much time for breakfast, but I had cinnamon toast on the drive.

Mother and I had moved to Pineview the summer of 1954 after Father died in a car crash. I met Miranda and Josie, which made the transition easier. Megan and her parents moved here near the end of the summer when Uncle Joe took over the management of Snow's General Store when Mr. and Mrs. Snow retired. I went to Miranda's eleventh birthday party on the long weekend where I met some of the other girls.

Megan's husky voice brought me back to the present. "Miranda is waving at us." Megan's brown shoulder length hair was held back with a wide turquoise hair band that matched her dress.

I skip-walked to keep up with Megan's long strides while we hurried to meet Miranda at the end of the sidewalk.

"Miss Grayson just came out and will ring the bell soon." Miranda's pony tail bounced up and down as we approached the yellow schoolhouse. She wore a pink dress with a full skirt with matching barrettes in her hair.

Groups of children gathered in front of a gnarled maple tree chatting. The yard sounded like a busy beehive until a bell rang and everyone rushed towards the steps. We arrived breathless and followed the others into the school.

I tucked my unruly reddish blond hair behind my ears while I paused in the doorway and gazed around the room. Two cloakrooms flanked each side of the door- one for the boys and one for the girls. It was different from what I was used to. This school consisted of 25 students while the class in my school, in Oak River, had 15 just in my grade.

Miranda had told me in Pineview school one teacher instructed all students from grade one to eight. My new class consisted of four students—Miranda, Megan, Jeff and me. We made our way down the aisles between the long rows of desks that faced the front of the room. The younger children sat in the front, with the oldest at the back. There was the sound of shuffling feet as we stood to sing "O Canada" and recite the Lord's Prayer. Some of the students glanced at Megan and me as we took our seats again.

Our teacher, Miss Grayson was tall and slender and wore a freshly laundered blue floral dress with her straight sandy blond hair cut in a fashionable bob. "I want to introduce you to our new grade five students, Bess Silver and Megan Skye."

"Good morning," they said, looking at us.

Miss Grayson paused when taking the attendance. "Does anyone know why Mike and Jeff Lambert aren't in school this morning?"

No one answered, but a few students shook their heads. Paper rustled, and pencils scraped as we copied assignments from the blackboard behind the teacher's desk.

We were doing our lessons when Mike and Jeff burst into the room.

"Why are you late?" Miss Grayson looked up from the book she was reading to the grade ones.

"Sorry. Father had an emergency with a cow, and we had to help." Mike strolled forward and handed her a note.

"No excuses. Take your seats," Miss Grayson picked up her fountain pen and made a note in her black attendance book.

"Umm, where do I sit?" Jeff glanced around the room.

"There's an empty desk in front of me," I heard snickers from the back of the room as Jeff walked to his desk.

"Take your seat. Your assignments are on the blackboard," Miss Grayson turned towards the grade ones. "You are disrupting everyone."

I looked up from my assignment to watch geese fly across the baby blue sky. The only noise was the honking geese and scraping of pencils. I watched one of the older boys pass Jeff a note when a bell rang. Jeff scowled and glared at the grade seven boy.

"Psst. Bess, it's time for recess." Miranda closed her books and stacked them neatly on the desk corner.

"Already," I closed my books and followed Miranda to the cloak room. Miranda wore one of her grandmother's creations. The full skirted pink dress had a wide white belt and collar.

Excited voices filled the air, with everyone discussing assignments and summer activities. The younger girls gathered around Megan and me, asking questions about living in Oak River.

We walked across the veranda and down the steps. "Tell us about your old school," Hope, a grade four student asked.

"It was a large two-story building with eight class rooms. My classroom was the size of this entire school with 15 students," I answered. "There were several teachers."

Hope twirled her red skipping rope in circles. "You walk awkwardly. How come?"

"I had polio." I pushed my long bangs out of my eyes.

"How awful. Weren't you scared?" Hope pushed her black framed glasses with thick lenses up.

"Yes." I polished my apple on my white blouse with embroidery on the collar. "I'm famished." Hope's long brown hair framed her oval face, and the thick lenses gave her eyes an owl-like appearance.

"Can you skip?" Hope asked.

"Not very well." I chewed on my lower lip as I looked at the inquisitive girls.

"Coming Josie?" Hope grabbed her friends hand.

Miranda, Megan and I sat under the gnarled maple tree watching the girls skip. Miranda spread out her full pink skirt with her dainty hands.

"The questions will die down in a few days. The little girls are curious about city life. Most of them haven't been far away from home."

I took a bite of my apple and turned to see what was causing the commotion.

"Jeff, do you want to skip with the girls?" Dan Holloway, a grade seven student taunted the younger boy.

Jeff put up his fists. "Do you want to eat dust?" His freckles stood out on his face, with auburn hair covering his eyes.

"Jeff has a girlfriend. Jeff has a girlfriend," Dan said in a singsong voice. His grin spread from ear to ear, and his hazel eyes sparkled with mischief as he brushed dark brown hair back from his face.

"Take it back," Jeff said, his face as red as his hair.

"Tough guy, are you?" Dan stood with his hands in fists with his feet shoulder width apart.

"Fight, fight," the boys chanted as they crowded around.

Mike pushed his way through the circle. "Cool off," he said, restraining his little brother.

"Let go," Jeff struggled to get free of the firm grip on his arm.

"You'll be in trouble at home for fighting. Let's play catch," his older brother said.

"All right." Jeff shuffled his feet and kicked up dust and followed his brother to the baseball diamond.

The excitement died down, and children gathered in little groups around the playground. Megan and I followed Miranda down a path toward the trees behind the outhouse. The grass swayed in the slight breeze and butterflies and dragonflies fluttered in the air ahead of us. Children ran and played, filling the air with excited voices. "What an interesting spot." Megan leaned over to tie the laces on her white and black shoes before she looked at the tables, made of wooden planks on top of tree stumps in a clearing in the maples.

A wooden swing hung by coarse ropes from a thick branch. Miranda hopped on it and started moving her legs back and forth, making the swing go higher and higher. Her black pony tail billowed out behind her.

4

She gradually slowed down, dragging her feet on the ground until she came to a complete stop. "This is our special spot."

Josie pointed to an area on the other side of the trees where tall grass was growing. "Let's make a house in the grass." She grabbed Hope's hand. "Come on."

The fourth-grade student held back. "Aren't you afraid of snakes?"

"Your father told you that last summer because he wanted to cut the grass for hay," Josie said. "They're garter snakes and won't hurt you. They are more afraid of you than you are of them."

By then, Josie was stomping around in the grass, flattening a small square in the knee-high grass. "This is the living room."

"There's the warning bell," Miranda said. "Miss Grayson doesn't like tardiness. Let's hurry."

We lined up by the steps before heading into the classroom. Desks opened and closed, and paper rustled as we prepared for our assignments.

The rest of the day flew by as we worked on assignments and visited. When the dismissal bell rang the students hustled to leave for the day.

Megan and I paused on the sidewalk in front of the blue bungalow Mother had purchased last summer. The house was set back from the street and surrounded by lilac and caragana hedges. "Are you coming over later?"

"As soon as I do my homework," Megan fiddled with the buckle on her blue book bag. "Mother and Father are strict about that. They weren't impressed with my marks last year."

I turned toward the house. "Okay. See you later." Megan and I had both failed last year. I had missed so much school when I was ill, but Mother made sure I did some catch-up work.

I plopped my book bag beside the doorway on the black and white linoleum floor. Herb pots soaked up light on the window ledge. The smell of garlic, basil and rosemary wafted off the tomato sauce. A pot of bubbling water sat on the stove. Spaghetti for supper, my favorite. The smell of fresh baked bread over powered the other smells.

"Oh, yum."

"How was your day, lassie?" Gramma asked in her soft musical voice.

"Interesting." I hugged Gramma; I was now glad that she had moved in with us last summer. Gramma had a bubbly jovial personality just like I'd imagined Mrs. Clause would be like. Her new short hair style framed her round face making her look younger.

"How so?"

"Mike and Jeff Lambert were late." I sliced a thick crust and slathered it with butter, watching it melt. "Jeff almost got into a fight with Dan, but Mike intervened."

"Why was that?" Gramma wiped her hands on her gingham apron.

"He didn't want to sit with the rest of the class—that consisted of girls." I took a big bite of my bread, picked up my navy book bag and walked awkwardly down the hallway with Pumpkin, my orange longhaired cat, at my heels, with his tail held high like a flag. My bedroom looked like a tornado had struck—clothes flung across the rumpled bed, chair and window seat. I looked around, shrugged and sat at the white desk. I cleared off the left side and took out my notebook and pencil.

I chewed on my pencil, trying to think of something to write for my homework assignment about my 1954 summer vacation. I did not know what to write. I doodled on the paper as my thoughts drifted back over events. Mother and I had moved here and Mrs. O'Toole, who I now call Gramma, moved in with us. I met Josie and Miranda, adopted Pumpkin, and I learned to walk without a crutch. I grinned and started to jot down my ideas.

My Summer
One: Megan's visit
Two: Picnic

Good, that is a start. I pushed my notebook to one side before picking up my heavy piggy bank lying beside the desk. In a few minutes, the dirty clothes were in the wicker laundry basket and clean ones hung in the antique oak wardrobe. Pumpkin paced back and forth swishing his tail while I made my bed.

"Hungry?" I turned toward the door and walked down the hallway as Pumpkin dashed past.

Later that evening, I arranged colorful patchwork cushions in a corner of the window seat and Pumpkin snuggled on my lap. Gramma made all the pillows over the years and gave them to me last summer. I looked at the new one with embroidered pansies in the middle which was my favorite flower. I had a book open but hadn't turned the page for the last 10 minutes. I glanced into the garden, where the trees were ablaze with orange, yellow and red. My thoughts went to all the things that had happened. The sound of a dog barking in the distance drifted in the open window.

Mother's voice brought me out of my daydream. "Time for bed." The scent of Jasmin filled the air as she kissed me on the cheek.

"In a minute." When I closed the green curtains, I noticed the streetlights had lit, illuminating the street beyond. It was quiet—even the dog quit barking. When I brushed my shoulder length hair, I glanced in the mirror. Freckles covered the bridge of my nose and cheeks giving an appearance of a tan. As soon as I slipped into my red flannel pyjamas, I snuggled into my sleigh bed while Pumpkin curled up beside me, purring.

***

The next morning came quickly, and Megan and I got to school with time to spare. After attendance, we started on our assignments. We had just finished our social studies when our teacher addressed the class. "There are a couple of committees to organize. Any volunteers for either the Athletic or Community Improvement committee?" Several students raised their hands. "One at a time," she said, pointing at Jeff, whose hand remained up.

"The Athletic Committee sounds like fun."

"Very good. Anyone else?" Miss Grayson asked.

Dan, in grade seven, and Robbie, in grade six, put their hands up. "We'll help with the Athletic Committee."

Miss Grayson wrote the names on the blackboard. "Who wants to organize the Community Improvement Committee?"

Miranda raised her hand. "What will the Community Improvement Committee do?"

Wrinkles formed in the corners of Miss Grayson's hazel eyes when she smiled. "You would be responsible for fall cleanup in yards and sprucing up rundown areas in town."

"I will help," Miranda said.

"Anyone else?" Miss Grayson looked around the room at the fresh, eager young faces.

Megan, Josie, Alice—in grade eight—and I put our hands up.

"Good—that's settled, then. Everyone dismissed."

***

The rest of the week flew by with homework every night. Miss Grayson didn't give us extra assignments for the weekend. I sat at my desk and took out my diary while Pumpkin curled up on the window seat.

September 1954

Dear Diary,

When Mother and I moved here last summer, I was hurt and resentful. I thought it wasn't fair that Mother wanted to move. Then I met Gramma. I started to like her and Pineview on the first day, even though I wouldn't admit it at first.

Gramma has lived in town for a long time and lost her husband last year, too. It was like this move was meant to happen, with Gramma becoming a member of our family. Mother says that family doesn't always have to be blood-related. I'd missed Megan—my cousin and best friend—and wrote regular letters. I was surprised when I learned her parents, Uncle Joe and Aunt Anna, had taken over the general store and bought a house down the street.

Miranda and Jeff are a year younger than Megan and me. I missed so much school when I was sick that there wasn't any way of catching up. I celebrated my twelfth birthday in the hospital with Mother, Father, Aunt Anna, Uncle Joe and Megan.

Megan's marks weren't that good last year, and Uncle Joe and Aunt Anna decided to hold her back a year. It doesn't seem to make much difference here because students of all ages hang out together. It is fun playing with younger children. I like helping them with their reading. The grade one and two girls like to play school in our special area in the schoolyard.

I don't know why I was so nervous and worried about going the first day. Everyone has been friendly. I still walk awkwardly at times, especially when I'm tired.

Last summer didn't start out that good when we moved here. I was still wearing a brace and using a crutch because of being in the final stages of polio. I felt self-conscious when people looked at me. Now I am fully recovered and walking normally most of the time. I am glad that it is all behind me and I can look forward to the school year and all kinds of fun things.

This afternoon Mother, Gramma and I went to the movie theatre. They played "Trigger Jr." starring Roy Rogers and Dale Evans. The Mickey and Minnie Mouse cartoons were hilarious. Gramma and I laughed so hard our sides ached. We got popcorn and soft drinks at the concession booth. Everyone comes to town on Saturday to shop and watch a movie.

We still have to bring in the pumpkins and squashes from our garden. Gramma preserved the apples and gave most of them away. She did not want anything left on the tree because they attract wasps.

I like the new furniture arrangement in my room. A couple of weeks ago, Pat Anderson, of the Anderson Construction Company, moved my bookshelves and placed one on each side of the window seat. Gramma and Mother asked him to make them look like built-ins. The bookcases extend to the ceiling with a shelf above the window. It is a cozy nook and my favourite spot for reading. Mother saw something similar in a magazine, and it gave Pat something to use as a design.

Our lives changed forever when Father died in that car accident last year. Our lives have settled down now, but there are times when I think about him, and it feels like it just happened yesterday.

I overheard Gramma talking about Miranda and her mother, Ava. Tom Anderson is doing repairs on their house free of charge. Gramma had said Ava and Tom were engaged.

Pat is here frequently. He mows the lawn and does repairs in the house for Mother and Gramma. He tells funny stories which lift our spirits when Mother and I are feeling sad.

Chapter 2 Discovering the Hidden Cabin

I nestled against a pile of colorful patchwork cushions on the bench, with a high back behind the oak table, late in the afternoon a few days later. Gramma sat on a stool in front of the blue counter, as she peeled the last few apples for a pie. I looked up from my book to admire the fresh bouquet of golden rod, daisies, mint, and ferns.

Megan's wide grin almost touched her gold-framed glasses when she darted into the cheery kitchen. "Father took the plaster off the kitchen wall, under the back stairs, and discovered a window! When Father and I peeked inside, we saw what appeared to be a room, but it's an old cabin." Megan paused to get her breath before continuing. "A stone fireplace covers the end wall." She stretched her arms wide to emphasis her words.

"A cabin? How is that possible?" I looked at the embroidered pansies on the tablecloth as Megan continued.

"Father thought the layout was strange. The house seems larger outside than inside," Megan waved her hands around.

Gramma paused with an apple in her hand. "I always thought the house looked bigger on the outside. There are a lot of odd angles at the back."

"When we explored your upstairs that rainy afternoon, we discovered a small door hidden behind that alcove. You and I could stand up straight in the small room that appeared to be an attic. There were exposed beams with log walls and a rough lumber floor," I rubbed my forehead as I tried to envision a small cabin.

"That is what made Father suspicious, and he started to investigate." Megan paused and snatched a slice of apple, only to get her fingers smacked. "There is also a crawl space from the spare room that leads into another storage area. The door slid open after a few tries, but the floorboards are loose with large cracks between them. It is impossible to

11

see below without a flashlight. Father threw out all the junk and said the floor wasn't safe to walk on."

"It sounds like a dark, gloomy space. Could the floor be a roof?" I shook my head in bewilderment taking in the information.

"Father sawed through the thick logs to gain entrance. It was hard to see in the dim light, even with flashlights. Cobwebs hang from the ceiling, and a thick blanket of dust covers everything. The fireplace is like a cave, and I can walk right in. The foundation stones are sinking. Father will get someone to help restore it," Megan fiddled with a loose thread in her shorts.

I rubbed my hands together anticipating what it would look like. "What else did you find?"

"An old desk, suitcases, a trunk and a lot of dust," Megan said. "Father wanted to throw everything out, but Mother and I convinced him not to. It might be fun finding out who owned everything. Mr. Snow, who is on the historical committee, came to see Father. Father has to discuss his plans with the members at the next meeting. Mr. Snow recommended finding out who left everything and who built the cabin and when."

I put my book mark in my book before I set it down. "You'll have to show me."

"The suitcases and trunk were in an old cupboard." Megan moved patchwork cushions aside and sat on the bench. "Father will bring the suitcases over."

"Why would they have been left there?" I asked.

"I knew you'd be interested," Megan hugged a patchwork pillow. "You had fun figuring out those clues that were left in your garden last summer."

"Yes, and I found the secret compartment under my window seat that contained old dolls and drawings. What fun," I answered.

"Some of the houses in this area were built by pioneers." Gramma wiped her hands on her bone white apron.

"Father's project is much bigger than he thought. He wanted to knock out a wall and remake the back stairs," Megan tapped her fingers on the table.

I squirmed, thinking over all the information. "How strange. I wonder why they would be in a cupboard?"

"There is an antique, roll top desk that contained a few notebooks and a bunch of yellowed papers," Megan twisted a strand of hair around her finger.

"Whoever did it was clever," Gramma put the pie in the oven.

Uncle Joe came in with the two battered suitcases and books tucked under his arm. "Megan insisted that I bring these over for Bess. I was going to throw everything out because it could be just a lot of rubbish. Where do you want them?"

Gramma led the way down the hallway. "Our girl thrives on solving mysteries. Let's put everything in the spare room."

Uncle Joe set the suitcases down before putting the books on the dresser in front of the window. "Have fun. I have to go back and haul out the plaster. I'll bring the trunk as soon as possible."

"See you in a bit," Megan answered.

The corners on the black suitcase were chipped. The lid sagged in the middle with several cracks with one broken latch. The other latch was rusty and creaked when I opened it. There were scraps of wool fabric and a blanket covering layers of yellowed newspapers and pieces of brown paper. A stained lace tablecloth was at the bottom.

I wrinkled my nose as a horrible smell filled the air. "What's that smell?"

"Mothballs and cloves." Gramma walked across the room and opened the window. "Everything smells musty."

"This piece of wrapping paper has the name 'Abigail Morgan' in one corner, with a smudged address," I looked through the papers.

Megan looked at the dusty tan suitcase. The handles were fragile with exposed wire, and the surface had scratch marks with tattered edges. "It's heavy."

13

I wiped the dust away with my hands exposing the lids dull finish before I pried on the latches without any success. "It is locked. Now what?"

Gramma's round face creased into a jovial smile when she rummaged around in her large apron pocket and removed a hairpin. "My grandfather taught me how to pick locks. It has come in handy a few times." She wiggled the locks, and a few minutes later, they opened with a loud pop and squeak.

I stared at the old books. I realized my mouth was open and I had been holding my breath as I waited to see if Gramma could unlock the suitcase. She was full of surprises. "What a treasure."

The paper rustled when we sorted and piled everything in the middle of the spare room's floor.

"There were quiet plops and swishes as we sorted and piled books. The cawing of a crow came in the open window and the bedside clock ticked. There was an assortment of text books, notebooks, picture books, and novels.

"Some don't have covers, while others have broken spines. "I rubbed my itchy nose before I wiped my hands on my shorts.

"They stink," Megan wrinkled her nose in disgust.

"It's a mixture of a sweet smell—floral scent and vanilla." Gramma looked through the stack of books. "An old-book smell that I love."

"There are a couple of old cookbooks and small ledgers. What strange recipes. They all say a dash of this and a pinch of that. It says 'high heat' on some while others say 'medium heat.' Whatever does that mean? It would be hard to follow them and make anything." I opened a small black one with a coarse fabric cover sewn with string. The inside binding was falling apart, and the stained, yellowed pages were ragged and torn around the edges, with bent corners. "Listen to this."

Recipe for a Happy Day

Take a little dash of cold water. A little leaven of prayer.

A little bit of sunshine gold dissolved in the morning air.

Add to our meal some merriment. Add thought for kith and kin

And then, as a prime ingredient, plenty of work thrown in.

Flavour it all with the essence of love and a little dash of play.

Let a nice old book and peace complete the well-spent day.

Gramma grinned. "Who wrote it?"

"It says author unknown." I turned the first torn page.

"Maybe from a friend," Gramma said.

"All the recipes are written by hand, and each has a different signature." I turned the delicate, stained pages. "This little cookbook got a lot of use. Some pages are missing." I closed the small, battered book.

"Gramma, did you recognize any of those names?" Megan peered over my shoulder.

"There's a couple of familiar last names. Mrs. Snow is on the historical committee and will be interested. She might know who Abigail Morgan was. There are records dating back to the early pioneer days," Gramma turned towards the doorway. "I have to check on the pie before it burns. That pumpkin pie recipe is similar to mine. I could easily make that one."

"I'd better go home to see if Father needs help. Bess, can you come over?" Megan headed down the hallway.

"Go ahead, lassie. I haven't started to prepare supper. Take your time," Gramma grabbed a potholder and opened the oven door.

Later that evening, I sat at my desk and took out my diary.

September 1954

Dear Diary,

What an exciting afternoon! Who would have figured Uncle Joe would find a tiny cabin behind the walls in their house? Megan and I explored for a few minutes before supper but did not find anything else. It was creepy in the dim light, with cobwebs hanging off everything. I got goose bumps on my arms and stood still when I saw a slender, petite woman, wearing an old-fashioned dress, sitting in a rocking chair beside the fireplace with a small book in her lap. Who could she be? Did she live in the cabin? She disappeared in an instant but was as real as Megan. The air around the fireplace felt chilly. I had a hard time shaking the feeling of overwhelming sadness that filled the cabin. Megan did not feel anything unusual and says it was my imagination. She had said I looked dazed, with a weird expression on my face.

Mother took her car to the garage for repairs because it is always breaking down. They looked after it right away. We took in a movie and did our shopping. By that time, the car was ready.

We spend a lot of time at recess playing in our special place, in the trees behind the outhouse. It feels magical in the dappled shade with grass, wildflowers, and ferns growing in abundance. It is always something different as we create games.

I cannot get that tiny cabin out of my mind. It is hard to imagine a family living there. There is one room with an enormous fireplace—their main source of heat and light. The fireplace stones are loose, and Uncle Joe will fix them. There does not appear to be a separate kitchen or bedroom. Uncle Joe and Aunt Anna want to turn it into a dining room.

I have been reading the old journals Uncle Joe left, but it is tough going because the pages are fragile and the writing is sloppy and smudged. So far, I have not found any major clues. I still have not figured out who Abigail was. Why did she live in the cabin? So far, more questions than answers.

Mrs. Snow, who used to look after the post office in the general store, dropped in for a few minutes after supper. When I asked her about Abigail Morgan, she had never heard that name before. She recognized some of the last names in the cookbook from the old town records. She was as surprised as the rest of us about the cabin. She suggested talking to Mr. Hub because his great-grandparents homesteaded near where he lives now. He might have heard stories and know something about the cabin. One of the names in the cookbook was Mrs. Zebedia Hub, who was Mr. Hub's great-grandmother.

I miss Father terribly and wish he were here. I am sure he would find something I have to be missing. He always loved solving a mystery. Father had been an elementary school teacher and helped me with homework. He had planned on tutoring me when I got out of the hospital before his life was cut short.

I stared into space with my chin cupped in my hands. I felt like I was talking to Father when I wrote in my diary. I feel like he is looking down with an amused smile, watching me struggle with clues. I closed my diary with a snap and put it back in the drawer.

Chapter 3 Finding Puppies

Ever since I saw that shadowy figure at Megan's, I have been having nightmares. Each time I walked along a path that twisted and turned through trees as thick as the hair on a dogs back. It is hard to shake the weird feeling that envelopes me each time. Why were the dreams haunting me each night? Last summer my visions contained clues that led to a hidden compartment under my window seat.

The week dragged by and I thought Friday would never get here because Miss Grayson had told us we would go on a nature walk. I listened to birds chirping and gazed out at the wispy clouds in the pale blue sky, unable to concentrate on my arithmetic assignment. My thoughts wandered to the old cabin and the notebooks. Who was Abigail? Why were her things in the old cabin? Miss Grayson's gentle voice brought my mind back to the present as she dismissed us for recess.

"Join us in a game of Anti-i-over," Miranda tossed a red and blue ball into the air.

I glanced at her for a minute. "What's that and how do you play?"

Hope dashed past. "Make way for faster traffic."

"It's easy," Miranda bent over to smell a goldenrod near the path. "Didn't you play Anti-i-over in Oak River?"

"No." I knelt down to take a pebble out of my shoe.

Miranda explained the game as we walked across the playground. "We need two teams and a ball." She put her hand over her eyes to shield them from the sun. "The more players, the better."

Other girls joined us as we strolled along the path worn in the grass from years of children walking through it. "The captain of the opposing team decides which side of the outhouse they want. Someone on the other side throws the ball over the roof. When someone catches it, she has to run around and tag as many players as possible that join their team. The group with the most players at the end wins."

Once we reached the outhouse, we formed two teams with five on each side—Miranda was on one, and I was on the other. I heaved the ball and was poised to run if someone caught it. I heard the ball land with a thud and the sounds of footsteps and giggles as they searched for it.

"Here it comes!" Josie said. She dashed forward to catch the ball and ran around the outhouse, tagging three girls who then joined our team. "It's our turn to toss the ball. Bess, you made a good throw last time."

In a few minutes, Hope sprinted around the corner and tagged me right away because I couldn't run fast. She touched three other girls, and we joined Miranda's team.

We played until the warning bell rang. Miranda's team had the most players. We were out of breath when we ran up to the veranda steps just as the second bell rang.

That afternoon, somewhere outside, a coyote howled. I looked up from my social studies and shuddered, thinking what it was like years ago when wolves roamed the nearby woods. As I looked out the window, I heard the distant tap tap of a woodpecker. Miss Grayson's voice brought me out of my daydream.

"Everyone put your books away. We will spend the rest of the afternoon outdoors." She set canvas bags on the front desks. "Take one and pass the rest back. Leave your homework assignments on your desks. When you are ready, line up in pairs by the door."

"Let's go together," Josie said as we walked to the girl's cloakroom.

"Sure, let's." I put on my beige sweater with a red rose pattern on the back before picking up my canvas bag.

Hope pushed out her lower lip into a pout. "Come with me. Not her."

I shrugged. "It doesn't matter. We are all going together."

The grass crunched under our feet as we walked across the schoolyard towards the nearby Woodland Historical Park. Our voices rose in excitement as we strolled single file along the narrow path under trees that sounded like a bird hotel. I looked up as a squirrel scolded and paused for a minute to listen to the sound of twirling leaves as the gentle breeze lifted them in the air.

Twigs snapped under out feet as we hiked through tall trees that almost touched the sky. Sun peaked through the leaves creating dappled shade and flickering shadows. The wind rustled through the leaves carrying the scent of wild mint and other herbs. Pinecones were scattered at our feet looking like little jewels. I almost bumped into Josie when she stopped abruptly in front of me.

"Why did you stop?" I put my hand on the rough, cracked ridges of a tree trunk to regain my balance.

"Listen. There's whimpering by the trees." Josie stood there with a handful of pine cones, listening. "Let's check it out."

"Be careful," Miss Grayson said. "It could be a wild animal."

"I'll go." Jeff leaped over a rotten tree trunk and almost slipped on squishy mushrooms. The mossy ground near the decomposing tree trunks muffled his footsteps. He waved. "Come over and look! It's a cute cocker spaniel and her puppies. Who would abandon them and leave them in a basket to fend for themselves?"

"They're so cute," Josie picked up the littlest one that squirmed and licked her face.

"Miss Grayson, come look," I knelt in the soft leaves petting their silky fur and scratching between their ears.

Hope held back and looked from a safe distance. "Will they bite?"

Miss Grayson looked at Hope's anxious face when she knelt beside her. "They are scared. Come, let's see if they are hurt."

Hope reached out gingerly to touch the little dogs silky fur. The dog gave an eager bark and licked her hands. "Aw."

Miss Grayson put her arm around the little girl's shoulders as they petted the mother dog. "The poor dears. Who would do such a thing?"

"Who will look after them?" Jeff cuddled the biggest of the litter. "The water and food is almost gone."

"Miss Prate's home and studio is nearby on the edge of the park near the river. We can ask her," Miss Grayson picked up the basket as she stood up.

We continued along the winding path in the dim light, through trees that towered high above our heads. At the edge of the meadow, I watched a couple of rabbit's zig zag through the feathery grass. Miss Grayson pointed out the log cabin nestled under oak and elm trees with red and rusty leaves.

We followed Miss Grayson into a cluttered room with exposed beams. "Sorry to barge in on you like this, but a dog and her puppies had been left in a basket in the woods. Could you look after them until they are old enough to go to homes?" She looked at a painting of a log building. "Is that the old sawmill?"

"Yes, it is," Miss Prate put her brush down. "Of course, I'll look after the little darlings. I heard someone tramping around when I was out painting this morning. Didn't see who it was, though. The little dog and puppies might not have survived overnight. I heard coyotes last night."

My mouth hung open as I gazed at the painting of an eagle. I almost reached out to touch it to see if it was real. "Mother bought your painting of the old Preston house, where we live. I am glad to meet you." Miss Prate's gray hair was in a bun at the nape of her neck. She wore denim coveralls—smeared with paint—over a blue shirt.

"I am glad you liked the painting. When I close my eyes, I can envision things the way they used to be. I have a photographic memory. The little dog and the puppies will be good company," Miss Prate said with a smile. "For the painting of the sawmill, I used some of my great-grandfather's preliminary sketches and notes so I wouldn't miss any details."

"Did you ever hear of Abigail Morgan?" I looked at the realistic painting. A golden light shone through the trees, illuminating two teams of horses pulling a heavy log out of the forest. Four men sat on top of the log, almost looking like miniatures. My eyes followed the path toward the two-story sawmill, built with roughly cut logs. A stone ramp led up to the open first-floor door with a pile of massive logs in front. In the distance, a log cabin and other buildings were cupped against the tree-covered hills.

"Can't say I have. Why do you ask?" Miss Prate answered as she put her paintbrush down.

"Uncle Joe was taking the plaster off the kitchen wall and found a window. He found suitcases and a trunk after sawing a hole in the exposed logs. What he thought was a room are the remains of an old cabin," I handed a squirming puppy to Hope.

"That house stood empty for years, and I was glad someone bought it. I didn't have any idea about another cabin hidden inside," Miss Prate answered. "Sorry, I can't help unravel that mystery."

"Do you need any help with the puppies?" Miranda struggled to hold a squirming pup.

"How about you kids find homes for them as soon as they are old enough to leave their mother?" Miss Prate answered. "Let's get them settled in. I have a corner that will work."

"We can bring dog food after school," Robbie and Jeff said almost simultaneously.

"Thank you. I would appreciate that," Miss Prate answered. "Would you like a tour of the studio?"

"Yes, please." We crowded around Miss Prate as she drew the outline of a fox with her brush before blocking in the background. We followed her around the room and looked at portrayals of birds, animals, and buildings on a variety of odd-shaped pieces of bark and wood.

Josie and I wandered around, looking at the representations of colourful butterflies, and birds that looked like they could take flight any moment. We dashed to catch up as the other students started toward the door.

For the next half hour, Miss Grayson gave us a tour around the outside of the old dilapidated sawmill.

"Some of the boards are missing in the front," Miranda gazed at the decaying logs and peeked through the cracks between the unpainted boards. "There is still equipment inside."

"This side stands straight, but the other side leans inward." Jeff jogged around the corner. "Some of the stones and logs are crumbling."

"It won't take much to bring it down," Miranda turned away from the crumbling building.

"Children, be careful. Jeff—it isn't safe to go inside. The building looks like it will fall at any moment," Miss Grayson said. "Let's continue."

Sticks snapped under our feet as we walked single file along the narrow winding path through the tall pine trees.

"Wasn't it Indians who originally made some of these old trails?" Jeff watched squirrels play tag up a tree trunk.

"Yes, it was," Miss Grayson answered as we paused at the base of a pine tree.

"Is this what it used to look like?" Josie looked at the animal trails that disappeared in a pile of leaves. Mushrooms and toadstools grew behind a clump of bluebells, daisies, and goldenrod with blue butterflies and white moths fluttering among the flowers.

"Yes, it is," Miss Prate and her cousins, Rae and Mae Prate, own the property. Their great-grandfather built it, and Miss Prate's father closed the mill when his brother passed away. Business was bad at the time because it was easier to obtain lumber elsewhere. They are going to have the old sawmill torn down before someone gets hurt," Miss Grayson said.

The fun-filled afternoon was over too soon, and we headed back to the classroom to put our things away and collect our homework.

When I got home, Mother and Gramma had company. Mothers best rose tea set looked pretty on the bone white table cloth. I inhaled the scent of mint and chocolate cookies. Mother set her cup down. "Bess, I would like you to meet Sadie Dale, who works with me at the hair salon. Her family has lived in the area for several generations."

"Your mother has been telling me about the old ledgers, trunk, and hidden cabin. Sadie dunked a chocolate cookie in her tea before taking a bite.

"It's a mystery." I poured milk into a blue glass. "I have asked several people if they had heard of Abigail Morgan, but so far, no one has. She almost seems to be a phantom."

"I have to admit that I haven't paid much attention to the old family names of those who settled the area. I will try to remember to ask Father. He has kept family records and loves doing genealogy research for our family and neighbours." The wooden chair scraped the floor when Sadie stood up. "The Hubs are another old family, and Mr. Hub might be able to shed some light on it. I don't remember much about the stories Mr. Hub and Father told."

September 1954

Dear Diary,

Our nature walk with Miss Grayson was a fun way to end the month. It was a good distraction from my research into the old cabin and inhabitants. The bad thing was the abandoned puppies and their mother. Megan, Miranda and I put posters around town and in the general store. No one has come forward claiming them. The month was full of fun things. It still feels like summer which makes it hard to concentrate on school work. We have been busy with all kinds of new and exciting projects.

I have been going through the old notebooks that are mostly an expense account and a record of important events in the area. I showed one to Pat when he came over to fix our clogged kitchen sink. He compared the prices to modern day costs.

Gramma had ladies over for tea this afternoon, and they love to gossip. I heard more interesting tidbits about Ava, Mothers boss. She has raised Miranda by herself after her husband died during a flu epidemic. What a sad story.

Ever since Megan showed me the old cabin in their house, I have been having recurring dreams. Each time I am walking on a narrow path that snakes its way through tall trees that block out the light. Each time I am looking for something but never find it. I wake up with a weird feeling every morning that is hard to shake. I haven't shared my dreams with anyone because I am not sure who to confide in. The last I saw a newly erected cabin, with a fire burning outside, near a meadow. I heard howling wolves just before I woke up.

Chapter 4 Talking to Mr. Hub

On Saturday morning, I helped Gramma pack a picnic basket while we waited for Megan and Josie. We were picking up Miranda on the way to Mr. and Mrs. Hubs' house. Alice was going to meet us because she did house cleaning there every Saturday. Since we were members of the Community Improvement Committee, we were going to rake the leaves in the Hubs' big corner lot. I had everything loaded in our blue station wagon when Josie and Megan arrived.

Mother stopped the car in the Hubs' driveway. "I'll pick you up at three."

"It's only ten which leaves us lots of time." I started to take the rakes out of the station wagon and leaned them against an oak tree beside Alice's red bike. When we had finished unloading, I gave Mother a hug and handed the picnic basket to Alice when she joined us.

Megan and I had finished raking the leaves from under the bushes and trees when there was a soft plop. I turned to see Josie laying with her arms and legs spread out in the middle of the large pile of red, gold, orange and yellow leaves with a toothy grin.

Megan stood with a rake in her hand. "What is she doing?"

"Playing by the looks of things." I wiped my dirty hands on my jeans. "Let's join her."

We took a break and started throwing leaves at one another until Alice approached. "Mrs. Hub wants to know if you guys are ready for lunch? She had started to set the table when I came out."

I giggled as I brushed leaves from my hair. "Gramma packed some scrumptious goodies in that basket for us to share with Mr. and Mrs. Hub."

"We need to cover the perennials and strawberries," Alice set the large wicker baskets beside the pile of leaves. "It shouldn't take long."

We filled the baskets and carried them across the yard to the gardens. The rest of the leaves would go into the wooden compost bin. We brushed the leaves off before heading toward the little white cottage.

We trooped into the old-fashioned kitchen with a square oak table in the middle. The ceiling sloped over the sink in front of the window, with geraniums on the wide sill. Mrs. Hub had the table set with white dishes on a red gingham tablecloth. There were a platter of sandwiches and a bowl of salad, with embroidered napkins at each place. A bowl of fruit sat in the middle of the table.

"Please help yourselves to whatever you like. You have been working hard all morning and must be hungry. Gramma O'Toole has prepared delicious treats, as usual. Mrs. Hub placed a plate of tarts, cookies and a brown tea pot on the table. It is nice to hear youthful chatter and laughter. It can get mighty lonesome at times, especially when Mr. Hub is out." Mrs. Hubs' crooked fingers gripped her ornate cane.

"Megan, I heard your father is doing some work on your house," Mr. Hub placed a ham sandwich and salad on his plate.

"Yes, he is. He found a few unexpected surprises," Megan helped herself to a ham sandwich and a pickle.

"The old desk contained journals that are mainly records of household expenses and other daily things," I took a bite out of an egg salad sandwich.

"Well, I recollect something about that old cabin." Mr. Hub stroked his white goatee for a minute. "When I was a boy, it was everything from a fort to a hideout. It was easy to gain entrance. All I did was pull on a piece of leather that opened the door." He took a few bites of his sandwich and salad.

"We haven't found the door yet. There doesn't appear to be an outside entrance," Megan's fork clattered as she set it down.

"Why, yes—The door was never locked. What fun we had. We pretended to be pioneers and would catch fish and cook them over a campfire. When the new owners moved in, everything changed." Mr. Hub rubbed his round belly.

"Did you remember if a trunk and suitcases were inside?" I asked.

"Several items were piled in a corner which included a locked suitcase. The trunk contained women's things that didn't interest us," he answered.

"When they moved, they must have intended to return for the rest but forgot," Megan folded her cloth napkin and took a sip of lemonade.

"Possibly. A No Trespassing sign went up when the new owner started building an addition." He took a sip of tea. "I often watched from a lofty perch in a pine tree. His wife and family joined him shortly afterwards. I tried to be friendly to his boy, but he wasn't interested in our games. I flirted with one of the girls, but she snubbed me." He dunked a gingerbread cookie in his tea and took a bite. "I think the new owner still used the cabin. I watched from my lofty perch while they constructed the roof. It remained intact at that time, and I heard he used it for a workshop."

"Have you ever heard of Abigail Morgan?" I wiped my mouth with my napkin, with roses embroidered in one corner, and pushed my plate away. "Who built the newer cabin?"

"I don't recollect any Morgan's in these parts," Mr. Hub answered, shaking his head. "Well—let me think—there might have been a Mr. Bennet, but I cannot be sure." He stroked his goatee before continuing. "Then one day they sold the place and packed up and left. I don't know why. I never paid much mind to local gossip. There wasn't any mention of the little cabin until now? There have been many people living there over the years. Maybe the outside logs were covered up with new ones, but I couldn't say for sure."

We sat around the table while Mr. Hub talked about his boyhood, but he never said anything else about the cabin. It seemed strange that no one had ever heard of Abigail Morgan. Someone must know something.

Mrs. Hub and Alice started to clear the table. "Are you just about done out there?" Mrs. Hub asked.

"Almost," I answered. "Mother will be here soon, so we need to finish."

We were just putting the baskets away when Mother drove up an hour later. "Are you ready? We can drop Alice off on the way home. Put everything in the car. I will pop in and say hello to Mrs. Hub."

"Just about," I stacked the last wicker baskets.

Alice moved her bicycle away from the tree. "I am finished inside and I will be going now too."

I stood with the rakes in my hand. "Do you want a ride? We can put your bicycle in the back of the station wagon."

"Thanks. I'd like that," Alice said.

When Mother came out of the house, we had everything packed and were waiting in the car.

***

Later that evening, I snuggled in the cushions on the window seat with Pumpkin cuddled beside me. My thoughts drifted to what Mr. Hub had said. Who was Abigail? Someone must have known her. So far, she almost seems like a phantom.

I shook my head, went to my desk and took my diary and pen out of the drawer.

October 1954

Dear Diary,

It was an exciting Saturday. We started our Community Improvement Committee projects. We split into small groups and made a good start. Did those things all belong to Abigail, or did some of them belong to the next people who lived in the cabin? I will have to look to see if there is a name on the old ledgers. Maybe there is something in there after all.

There are times I miss Father intensely. It hits me when I am not expecting it. I often see a sad look in Mother's eyes. I would love to be able to share everything with Father. When I write in my diary, I feel like I am talking to him.

29

Chapter 5 Opening the Trunk

I was having a hard time concentrating on my homework because my thoughts wandered to the unanswered questions about the old cabin. Pumpkin purred on my lap with his paws resting on the edge of the desk.

I thought about what Mr. Hub told us about the property. It was older than we had originally thought and built to withstand the test of time. The construction date was the early 1900s. Who built the cabin? Why did they leave? Where did they go? Did they vanish? No one has ever heard of any Morgan's.

I moved the ledgers out of view and tried to concentrate on homework. I tapped the floor with my feet before glancing at the clock beside my bed. Birds twittered outside the window and Pumpkin jumped down and ran over to the window seat and scratched on the glass. I sat with my pen poised in midair as I watched him. I decided that tonight was the time to open the old trunk—when Mrs. Snow, Aunt Anna, and Megan joined us after supper.

As soon as I finished my homework, I took out the last ledger. I flipped through pages of expenses and found a short note.

January 1920

Well, I will rit a few lines, to tell youse about my progress since starting at the mill. The work is steady due to the mild weather. There is plenty of work for everyone in the woods. Well, so far it is a pretty good winter but cold. I was fortunite to have found this sturdy little cabin that had been empty for awhile. I started to cut down trees for logs to make an addition so my family could join me. Could no, find information about the trunk and suitcases I had found, so I built a cupboard around them. Due to lack of time, I placed an add in the local newspaper and placed posters in local stores.

I skimmed through the pages of expenses and notes about events and dates. The writer talked about the construction of the new cabin and his wife and children arriving. Then another note caught my attention.

September 1920

Well, I have a few minutes so will scribble a few quick lines. It is terribly lonesome without the wife, the wee lassies, and lad. Now that the addition is complete they will join me soon. The oald cabin makes a good office and workshop. I created a hidden latch to the door in the oald cabin but haven't told anyone else where it is or how it works.

I put the ledger away. The handwriting was messy and looked like chicken- scratch across the page. When he made expense entries, it was neater, but his scribbled notes were difficult to read.

Gramma and Mother's voices in the hallway brought my mind back to the present. I entered the kitchen and inhaled the smell of roast chicken, gravy, potatoes, and peas. A chocolate cake sat on the counter. I was famished and hastened to set the table.

***

Mother and I had just finished the dishes when Megan, Aunt Anna, and Mrs. Snow arrived. We gathered around the large domed wooden trunk with its rusty hinges, brass corners and a broken lock that dangled. I flipped the latches up and opened the trunk, filling the room with a mixture of smells. "Megan, grab the other side of the tray so we can take it out."

31

"This is in good condition," Megan moved her fingers out from under the tray before she set it down. "Look! There's a second one."

Gramma and Mother took out the second tray while I opened the first one. "Look at the delicate handcrafted handkerchiefs and napkins." I ran my fingers over the napkins. "The initials J. D. are embroidered on everything, and the doilies have fancy patterns. Who is J. D.? I thought the name was Abigail Morgan."

"I haven't seen napkins made with Irish linen for years." Gramma sorted through everything. "These are all sewn by hand. She was an excellent seamstress."

I pulled out an old-fashioned satin peach dress, with long puffy sleeves with dainty glass buttons on the wide cuffs. "The cuffs are frayed, and the stitches are coming out."

"It's old," Gramma laid items back into the tray. "Maybe a hundred years old or more. Those clothes are all hand sewn with care."

"Hey, look." Megan, rummaging around in the trunk, pulled out black and white framed snapshots. "One looks like a wedding portrait, while the other is a group photograph. They all look stiff and formal, with such serious faces. You would think if it were a happy occasion, they would at least smile. Doesn't that dress in the picture look like the peach one?"

"Yes, it does." I continued to pull items out of the trunk and soon had a mound in the middle of the floor.

"In those days, it took a long time to pose for photographs. They had to stay still without even a twitch. Taking pictures was a serious undertaking—something new," Gramma answered.

Megan pulled out a small bundle wrapped in soft flannel. Gramma looked over her shoulder. "What do we have here?"

"It's embroidered pictures. One of a large house, and the other of two people sitting on a porch," Megan said.

"They are samplers. Young girls learned their embroidery stitches that way," Mrs. Snow said as she watched. "They are well done—the stitching is dainty and neat. Could have been her family. Girls often used their families as models for their work."

"The outside of the trunk looks bigger than it is," Megan looked through some of the items. "Doesn't that seem odd?"

I ran my hand along the paper that lined the bottom. I didn't find anything unusual at first, but I continued to investigate and found a leather tab. I pulled on it, and a board lifted out easily.

"Look at that," Mrs. Snow gestured as she talked. "Aren't you the one for finding secret compartments?"

I took out a small green clock and a black jewellery box. The lid creaked when it opened to reveal antique jewelry nestled on red velvet. "What a pretty locket and a delicate gold chain."

"These rolled-up papers were in the top tray," Megan said. "I wonder what they are?"

Paper rustled when I untied the ribbon and unrolled the fragile pages. "Looks like old letters or a journal. The writing is dainty and smudged. They will be hard to read."

"This is an old steamer trunk that could have been used to smuggle things out of the old country," Gramma said. "I have seen similar ones before."

"Goodness gracious," Mrs. Snow smoothed out the wrinkles in her green cotton dress. "What happened to the poor girl? I have never heard of anything like that before."

"Will the secret ever be revealed?" Megan asked.

"If anyone can solve the mystery, it's our Bess," Mrs. Snow leaned on the edge of the trunk as she stood up.

"Let's go look in the cabin again," I turned towards the doorway. While everyone else had tea Megan and I strolled hand in hand down the tree lined street."

***

Megan and I stood in the middle of the log cabin, looking around. My shoes clicked on the wide planks as I crossed the floor. "This must be an outside wall?" Where would the door be?"

"It has to be, but there isn't any sign of a door," Megan tiptoed across the creaky planks.

"Thankfully the cobwebs are gone. I hate spiders," I poked around in the spaces between the fireplace stones. Then, out of the corner of my eye, I noticed a slender woman standing beside the fireplace with a small book in her hand. She appeared to put it in a small crevice. Then she went to the door and pulled on a leather strap. The vision disappeared in an instant.

"What do you hope to find?" Megan leaned against the rustic pine mantel.

I walked along the fireplace, running my hand lightly over the stones and logs. At first, I didn't feel anything different. "I don't know for sure."

"You have that weird look on your face again. Are you all right?" Megan's brow wrinkled when she looked at me.

"I'm fine." I ran my hand over the logs in the corner. Then I noticed a tiny knothole in one of the logs. When I put my little finger inside, it wiggled. "Come here for a second. I think I found something!"

"What?" Megan held the flashlight and squinted in the dim light.

"There's a loose section in this log," I stuck my finger in the knot hole and pulled until it opened with a loud pop.

"Hey, look— a shelf with things on it," Megan shone the flashlight inside.

I pulled out a couple of books with hand-sewn leather covers and bindings. "The initials J. D. are embroidered on the cover." I felt around inside and found another bundle tied with faded blue ribbon.

"What made you look there?" Megan asked.

"A hunch," I left the little door open. "How clever." I continued to feel around hoping to find the leather strap for the door. At first, I didn't feel anything unusual. "Megan look!" I held the end of a stiff piece of leather. "That could be where the door is. Do you have something to mark the spot? Your Father will want to see this."

Megan dashed to my side and stared in disbelief. "Father had been over that wall several times without any luck. Hang on I'll get a yellow ribbon and a tack."

I shivered when I felt a slight breeze near the fireplace. "Let's go. Gramma was making hot chocolate."

"You've got goose bumps all over your arms," Megan answered. "You let your imagination get the better of you."

"It's not my imagination," I answered.

Megan stood in the bright kitchen and opened one of the journals. "How are you ever going to read that dainty writing?"

I peeked over Megan's shoulder. "Not easily. It's the same writing as on the loose pieces of paper. The writing in the ledgers is different." We walked down the street, with the streetlights creating shadows.

***

That evening, my thoughts whirled, making sleep impossible. The garden looked like an enchanted fairyland with the moonlight shining down. With the colourful, crazy quilt around my shoulders, I took out my diary and pen and sat cross-legged on the window seat.

October 1954

Dear Diary,

It is still a big puzzle. I have two diaries and loose pages to read. The writing is dainty and smudged, which will make it difficult to figure out. The initials J. D. were on the covers. Who is J. D.? It remains a mystery as to why they would move and not take their belongings with them. The items in the trunk belonged to a woman.

It has been an exciting weekend. Nothing like this ever happened in the city. What happened in that cabin?

Maybe someone will read my diary someday and try to figure out things about my life. The dainty handwriting does fit with the linens and things from the trunk. It was so different then—a rugged countryside with no towns anywhere nearby. It had to have been a rough life. It is interesting reading someone's life history.

Miss Grayson has been teaching Pineview history and geography. I can use material from the old ledgers and diaries in my written assignments. I am learning things Miss Grayson cannot teach me.

Father would have loved diving into this mystery. Mother had said I take after Great-Grandmother, who often predicted the future accurately. I have had glimpses into the past several times since moving here. It can be a bit creepy at times.

Chapter 6 Sports Day

Two weeks have passed since Megan, and I explored the old cabin and found the diaries and bundle of letters in a hidden compartment in the corner near the fireplace. I also found the leather cord for the door. Uncle Joe did some work on that wall and found the door but hasn't figured out how to open it. Something prevents it from opening. He can't alter it without permission from the historical committee. Uncle Joe talked to Mr. and Mrs. Snow and is waiting to hear back.

The growing excitement of our upcoming sports day pushed the mystery to the background for a while. Dan, Jeff, Robbie, Megan, Miranda, Alice and I stayed in at lunch to plan activities while Miss Grayson graded papers.

"Should we have a sack race?" Robbie closed his dented lunch pail.

I looked up from my notes. "Don't you think we have enough with the skipping competition, relay race, three-legged race and broad jumping?"

"That sounds like a good variety and will include everyone," Alice polished her apple on her mauve blouse.

"Good. I will write everything out and give it to Miss Grayson." I turned the page in my notebook.

"That takes care of the sports day, but what about the puppies?" Alice paused to take a bite of her sandwich. "Mr. Hub told me he saw a fancy sports car parked near the woods the day we found them. Whoever dumped them is long gone. There's been no response to the ad in the newspaper, or the posters we put up."

"Miss Prate is keeping one of the puppies." I continued to take notes. "Her cousins, Mae and Rae, might take it later."

"Mother and Father said I could have a puppy," Megan took an apple out of her lunch pail with baseball players on the lid.

"Mother said I could have one," Miranda wiped crumbs off her desk onto a cloth napkin.

"Good, all three puppies will have a home. Then all the business is taken care of," Alice closed her lunch pail. "Meeting adjourned."

"Robbie, do you want to play catch?" Jeff picked up his lunch pail and stood up.

"Sure do," Robbie put his thumbs under his red suspenders and strolled to the boy's cloakroom to put his lunch pail away.

***

It was hard to concentrate on schoolwork as we waited for sports day. But the time flew by, and soon the anticipated day was here. I snuggled under the covers, listening to the twittering birds. I slipped out of bed and got dressed. Today was a casual day, so I selected jeans, red blouse, and sneakers.

I had just finished breakfast when Megan arrived. "Ready? We are early, so let's walk."

"Good idea," I grabbed my lunch pail and book bag.

We walked along silently, each lost in our thoughts. The only sounds were the shuffling of our feet on the sidewalk, squirrels chattering and singing birds. The sun shone through the bare branches and remaining leaves, creating weird shadows.

It was a busy morning, and we had a break at noon after the skipping competition. The younger children were strutting around, showing off their ribbons.

After lunch, students started to line up for the three-legged race. They formed pairs and made a crooked line with their inside legs tied together with rope. They started awkwardly, but most were able to maintain their balance. Students ran diagonally across the path of others creating confusion. They fell and lay there giggling. They stood up with somber faces and proceeded with the race. For a while, it looked like Jeff and Robbie were going to win, but Josie and Hope started to catch up. The girls beat Jeff and Robbie to the finish line.

The race had ended when Miss Grayson rang the bell to get everyone's attention. We ran over to the veranda, with Josie and Hope showing off their red ribbons. We gathered around Miss Grayson.

"Thank you for all your hard work. There are prizes for the committee organizers. Miss Prate painted pictures of the puppies on round pieces of pine. Alice, Bess, Megan, Miranda, Josie, Robbie, Dan, and Jeff, come forward," Miss Grayson said.

Clapping and cheering filled the air as the other students congratulated the committee organizers. As soon as we collected our book bags, lunch pails and sweaters we followed Miss Grayson to the adjacent park to wind up the day with a wiener roast.

***

The street lights had started to come on when I got home, and I looked around my messy room. I started to hum as I picked up my dirty clothes and papers that were scattered everywhere. I sat at my desk, tapping my feet for a few minutes before taking out the loose pages we had found in the trunk. There had not been much time lately to think about the mysterious woman.

March 10, 1909

It had been a gloriously warm day, but that changed abruptly at nightfall when the temperature dropped dramaticlly accompanioned by snow. I had been certain it was spring but was sadly mistaken. It was picturesque with big snowflaks cascading from the dark sky against the back drop of green trees.

With my household chores done, I will take some time to record things for future generations.

It was a long, tiring trip across the prairie last summer. I travelled by train with a family who were settling near here. I left Mother and Father's in late August.

I listened to the constant rattling of the wheels, and it took a few days to learn to walk straight down the aisles. There was a small stove at the back of the car, and we took turns cooking small meals. It was hard to sleep with all the starts and stops along the way. The sky was a mixture of pink, and pale blue with fluffy pink edged clouds when the train chugged into Pineview. I was almost at the end of my long journey.

I rubbed my eyes as I gazed around and listened to the huzzle and bustle on the train platform as the passengers disinbarked. I shelded my eyes with my hand and finally spotted Jake waving as he dashed towards me. We collected my trunk and other luggage before taking them to the horse and buggy Jake had hired for the remainder of the trip. We stopped at the top of a hill while Jake pointed out our cabin cupped at the base of a tree covered hill. The view was magnificant with the green, yellow and red trees on the rolling hills.

Life is much harder here than it was at home. There, servants attended to our needs while here I am up at daybreak and work from dawn to dusk. The forest is full of wildlife which is a constant supply of fresh meat. Some of which I had never eaten before. It can be challengeing figuring out how to cook some of the different meats. If in doubt I always make a variety of stews.

Everyday I am serienaded by birds which is my only source of music, these days. It is a pleasure to step outside for a break and listen. I am learning to identify birds and small animals that abound here.

J. D.

I rubbed my eyes and yawned before putting the loose papers in the desk drawer. I jumped into bed when Mother's voice carried down the hallway. My thoughts wandered to J. D., and I wondered who she was. What a hard life. I nestled into the blankets with Pumpkin cuddled at my side. I soon drifted to sleep and dreamt about pioneers, trains, towering trees and log cabins.

The next morning after breakfast, I took out my white, gold-edged diary and pen and sat on the window seat to write.

October 1954

Dear Diary,

The barbicue, Miss Grayson held in the park, was a delightful surprise ending to our sports day. We got home late, and the street lights were coming on when I closed my bedroom curtains. It had been unusually warm for October almost feeling like summer instead of fall. Some of the parents came to help supervise and cook hotdogs and hamburgers. Uncle Joe gave a bunch of us a ride home. When I got home, I had a letter from, Mr. and Mrs. Mar, our old neighbours in Oak River. It was full of gossip about the kids from school and neighbourhood friends. It was great to hear from them.

I was surprised to find my window closed because I left it open last night. Mother must have closed it before she left for work. Gramma was busy with her usual Saturday morning chores when I got up.

It has been warm out for October. Gramma calls it Indian summer, but it was a bit chilly this morning, so I did not stay in the garden very long. It looks barren now that all the flowers are gone. Gramma says the weather will change—she can feel it in her bones.

Chapter 7 Halloween Party

On the weekend, I had some free time to take out the old diaries. During the week, I had been busy with schoolwork and activities. I felt bewildered after listening to Mr. Hub's tale and reading J. D.'s diary. Who was J. D.? What was her last name? Who was Abigail? I took out the loose diary pages and started to read. The dainty slanted writing was difficult to read. Was she left handed like me?

May 5, 1909

There have been several letters and packages from home. It has been a while since I have written anything and try not to waste paper because it can be scarce. Most nights I am exhausted and do not feel like writing.

My mother's and sisters letters are full of gossip and details about the functions they attend. Jake and I had a few neigbours over to help us celebrate the arrival of spring. The ladies brought preserves and receipts that they wrote in my grandmother's old cookbook. They helped me wash down all the inside logs to kill any surviving insects that might have lingered there over the winter. Jake will get some white wash the next time he goes to the General Store. The men helped Jake clear some more trees off the property. I have asked him to save any fruit trees they found.

The day ended with a big meal. Jake had a wild boar roasting on a spit over an open fire near the cabin. A lot of stories were shared and then we had a sing along around the fire.

The wolves constantly howl and get on my nerves. When I went to the creek this afternoon, I saw wolves near the edge of the forest making the hair on the back of my neck rise. I quickly got a pail of water and almost ran back to the cabin. Jake builds a large fire nearby, in the evenings, to keep the wolves away.

Yesterday's mail contained newspapers and a couple of letters—one from Mother and one from a dear friend. I've read the other ones so many times that I memorized them, and I can hear their dear voices when I read their letters.

Jake and I plan to plant the garden soon. Mother sent seeds in her last parcel. Our supply of vegetables is dwindling.

I shivered after putting the pages back into the desk drawer. How sad. I took out my notebook and made a few notes. I'm no closer to finding answers. Closing my eyes, I could envision J. D. writing out her thoughts at the end of a long day.

***

On Monday morning, we were finishing our assignments when Miss Grayson made an announcement. "There will be a Halloween party on Friday, with a potluck lunch and games."

"Do you want everyone to bring something special?" Megan twirled her pencil.

Miss Grayson smiled. "No, just bring what you normally do, with a little extra to share. Austin and Kyle Cross, identical twins, will be joining our grade five class in a few days."

Jeff grinned. "Not the only boy in the class anymore!"

Miss Grayson's grey eyes twinkled. "That's right; you won't be. Class dismissed." The room was full of the sound of desks opening and closing, shuffling feet and the buzz of everyone talking about the new classmates and the upcoming party.

***

Later that afternoon, I rummaged through my closet looking for costume ideas but didn't find anything. I paced back and forth, pausing to look at the old journal. Of course! A pioneer.

After supper, I was putting cutlery in the drawer. "I decided to dress as a pioneer for Halloween. What could I wear?"

"Well, let me think." Gramma pulled the plug and rinsed out the sink. "Let's go look in my trunk."

A few minutes later Gramma opened her large brown trunk and took out the tray lined with floral paper. She pulled out a navy long skirt and jacket. "These will work with a white blouse. Put your hair in a long braid and wind it around the back of your head."

I gave Gramma a hug before I went to my room with the outfit. "Thanks."

***

After a week of constant homework, it was Friday morning and the day of our Halloween party. It was quiet, with a few sounds coming down the hallway, which meant Gramma was up. Pumpkin's wet nose bumped against my cheek when I rolled over. "Today is our party." I hopped out of bed and ran over to the window. "Good—no clouds. It should be a good day after all. Maybe Gramma was wrong."

I looked in the full-length mirror as I adjusted my costume. The skirt almost touched the floor. The jacket fit snugly with just enough room for a short sleeved white blouse. Mother had braided my hair before she left for work. I looked elegant and grown up. I gathered up my books

45

and strolled to the kitchen that smelled of waffles, maple syrup, and bacon.

"You look just like a pioneer in that outfit," Gramma put a stack of waffles on a plate. "Here's the matching hat that I found late last night."

I was just finishing breakfast when Megan dashed inside. "Hey, are you ready?"

I pushed my plate away. "Yes." I grabbed my lunch pail, book bag, and parka. "I like your costume. You'd wear a baseball uniform all the time if you could."

"I am supposed to be Mickey Mantel. I like yours as well." Megan turned towards the door.

"Picture first." Gramma grabbed her camera off the counter. "It won't take long."

***

Moans and groans could be heard throughout the room when we were assigned arithmetic and spelling before our party. I had a hard time concentrating on sums and spelling rules, but managed to get everything completed and would not have extra homework.

Dark clouds had built up unnoticed during the morning while we had our heads bent over books. Now the clouds moved rapidly, and the wind picked up, swirling dust and leaves everywhere. We had just finished lunch when it turned as dark as night, even though it was only midday. The wind moaned and groaned outside, rattling the windows.

Miss Grayson turned the lights on as students ran to the window. The lights flickered off and on and finally went out. Miss Grayson spoke to the class. "The phone lines are down. Dan and Mike, run to the general store and see if you can arrange rides. It was such a nice morning that I had decided to walk. Everyone is safe here."

"Right away," Dan answered as he dashed to the boy's cloakroom.

"Be back as soon as possible," Mike struggled against the fierce wind that threatened to snatch the door out of his hand.

It was cozy in the little schoolhouse, but the wind howled outside. Miss Grayson clapped to get everyone's attention. "Do you want to play a few games until the boys come back."

"Let's play Red Light, Green Light," Miranda said. "Bess and Megan, do you know how to play?"

"Not sure," I answered.

"Okay, let me refresh your memory," Miranda said. "Everyone lines up at the back of the classroom, facing the front. I will stand in front of Miss Grayson's desk. When I turn my back to everyone, I will call out 'green light.' That gives you permission to move forward as quickly as you can. When I turn around, calling 'red light,' you have to stop. If you keep moving after I have shouted out 'red light,' you have to sit down. Everyone ready?" She looked around for a minute. "The one who gets to the front unseen and tags me wins. Let's go."

"Green light!" Miranda turned to face the front. In a few minutes, she twirled around, calling out, "Red light!" Everyone tried to stop balancing precariously and bumping into one another. "Jeff, Megan, and Robbie, you're out. Take a seat."

We giggled as we tried to balance in awkward positions. Miranda grinned before turning her back to us. "Green light!" Everyone dashed forward, hoping to tag Miranda before she turned around again. Then she twirled, saying, "Red light!"

Josie was almost beside Miranda but had to sit down along with five other students. "Almost made it." She gazed out the window and watched snow drift across the yard. "There are cars and trucks in the parking lot."

The door burst open, and Uncle Joe came in, bringing an icy blast with him. "Gather up your things. There are rides for everyone."

Tom Anderson struggled with the door when a gust of wind tried to grab it out of his hands. "It's bad out there. It will get a lot worse before nightfall."

Uncle Joe said, "Megan, Miranda, Bess, and Josie, come with me."

"Mr. and Mrs. Hub have room for students that can't make it home," Tom said.

"Mr. Snow and Pat are waiting outside to give rides as well," Uncle Joe said. "Dan and Mike are at the store; in case anyone needs anything."

We went to the boys' and girls' cloakrooms to bundle up before going outdoors. I pulled off the long skirt I wore over jeans and folded it before putting it in my book bag with the jacket and hat. We quickly bundled up and gathered in groups by the door.

Megan, Miranda, Josie and I held hands with the wind whipping our scarves around. Pellets of icy snow stung when they hit our faces as we struggled against the fierce wind. The five-minute walk to the car felt like an hour, and I was glad to pile into the backseat.

Uncle Joe drove slowly, with the windshield wipers going continuously. The snow swirled across the road, and the trees swayed back and forth. Even with the headlights, it was difficult to see where the road was, and the car almost went sideways a few times. We drove along in silence, holding hands, listening to the howling wind, the scraping of the windshield wipers and the hum of the motor as Uncle Joe struggled to keep the car straight.

***

An hour later, I entered our warm steamy kitchen.

I sat at the table with a cup of hot chocolate cupped in my hands. Steam twirled as it rose and the warmth seeped through my fingers. The snow swirled in circles, and tree branches scratched the windows. I gazed out the window at the blanket of snow covering the garden, where plants stuck out like skeletons. I pushed my cup away and headed down the hallway. When I reached my room, I shivered, even though it was warm and cozy, pulled the blind down and closed the curtains. It did not shut out the sound of the howling wind that rattled the windows, trying to get in through little nooks and crannies.

I turned my back to the raging storm, took the old frayed diary out of the desk drawer and started to turn the delicate pages. My thoughts wandered to J. D.

August 1909

I complained to Mother about the lack of writing paper the last time I wrote. What a surprise when Jake brought home a parcel that contained many of the household items I had been missing. A special surprise was this precious journal with my initials on the soft leather cover.

There have been several letters from my little sisters and Mother. I hung my sisters watercolors on the walls so I can see them every day. It cheers me up when I look at them. Occasionally I take the samplers they gave me as going-away presents out of the trunk. I do not want to hang them up because the smoke from the fireplace will ruin them.

There has not been a word from Abby. Will she ever forgive me? Can I help it if Jake fell in love with me and not her?

Mother was excited when she heard about my pregnancy, but worries about me being out here in the "wild frontier" where there are not any doctors within miles. The baby will arrive in late fall or early winter. We are excited, and I have been making little nighties and booties for him or her. I am also anxious about having a wee one out here.

Mrs. Knight, a neighbour, dropped in a few days ago. She is different than anyone I have ever met before. She was a tall, stalky woman wearing dark colored clothes made from homespun fabric. She carried a walking stick and a riffle. She warned me about the wild animals and not to travel by myself. Her voice was surprisingly gentle for a woman her size. She has eight children and has helped deliver babies. What a relief to know there is someone nearby.

I closed my eyes while I held the diary in my hand. I cupped my chin in the palm of my other hand while I thought about the things I had read.

I found myself walking down a narrow path toward a cabin in a clearing surrounded by dense forest. The same woman I saw by the fireplace sat on the step shelling peas, from a basket in her lap, while she rocked a cradle with her foot. A smile crossed her face. Did she see me? When I looked over my shoulder, a tall young man dressed in homespun clothing walked up the path toward her. Where was I? Was this Jake and J. D.'s cabin? I saw them, but they did not see me.

Noises coming down the hallway brought me back to the present. I felt weird for a second. Had I fallen asleep? Was it a dream? I shook my head as I put the diary back in the drawer.

Ten minutes later, I walked down the hallway toward the kitchen. I paused to admire the lacy pattern the frost made on the living room window. I scraped a small hole so I could see outside. Part of the town was in total darkness. The storm was getting worse, making it difficult to see across the street. Big snowbanks reached up to the windowsill. I entered the cozy kitchen and put the skirt, jacket and hat on the back of a chair.

"Supper is just about ready. There is a pot of soup and fresh baked bread." Gramma stirred the bubbling mixture as good smells filled the air. "At least our power is still on."

"I followed the smell down the hallway. It is so nasty out, and I hope everyone got home all right," I took bowls and small plates out of the cupboard.

Mother came into the kitchen. "I saw Uncle Joe's car pull into the drive way awhile ago. It's warm and cozy in here, even though it is miserable outside. I heard storms could be bad but didn't expect this."

***

It was quiet and peaceful the next morning, but it was still snowing. I ran over to the window and raised the shade. The garden looked magical under the thick blanket of snow. The tree branches bowed low with the weight of the snow, forming tunnels all over the yard. Big snowdrifts hid the stone wall. I tried to phone Megan, but the phone lines were still down.

A half hour later, I went into the kitchen to feed Pumpkin after peeking out a clear spot in the living room window. It was a winter wonderland. "I have never seen so many big snowdrifts."

"When the snow stops, there will be snowploughs out. The boys will start shovelling as soon as possible. It is fortunate your mother put the car in the garage," Gramma said as she set out bread to rise. "It would have been buried. We had a similar storm five years ago."

I had been helping Gramma and Mother with household chores for the last couple of days, with not much time to myself. I went to my room with a cup of hot chocolate and a chocolate muffin. I opened the desk drawer, took out my diary and pen and started to write.

November 1954

Dear Diary,

October came to a dramatic end with that violent snowstorm. The storm pretty much shut down the town. Uncle Joe wore snowshoes to get to the general store, but the beauty salon is still closed. Mr. Anderson, Pat and Tom's father, hitched his Clydesdales to a sleigh and gave some of the kids a ride home.

I have been working on the paint-by-number set I got early in the fall. It is a picture of a grey cat peeking out of blue pansies. It is going to be pretty. The second picture has a white cat surrounded by red roses. I have also been doing arithmetic homework at Mother's insistence.

Last night I had a dream where I was walking down the trail towards the cabin again. It was beautiful with all the wild flowers, tall grass and tree branches full of a variety of song birds. Their warbling sounded like an impromptu concert. Every time I feel strange when I wake up, and it takes a few minutes to shake the strange feeling.

Pat came over to see if we needed anything and stayed for a cup of coffee. He used snowshoes to get around. He shoveled the driveway which was a big help for Gramma and Mother.

Chapter 8 New Classmates

I snuggled among the colourful patchwork cushions on my double sleigh bed with a book open on my lap. Pumpkin lay beside me, purring, as I stared into space thinking about the things I had learned about the mysterious J. D. I had visions about the same woman wearing an old-fashioned dress and dreams where I was walking on a woodland trail. Everything felt strange and unbelievable. Who would believe me? Mother had mentioned something about my grandmother being able to predict the future. I seemed to have the ability to see into the past. Is it possible, or was I simply dreaming? I set my book aside and hopped down, landing with a thud.

I took the elusive J. D.'s diary out of the top drawer and opened it. I was surprised to see a letter flutter out and land on the desk.

To my dearest sister,

I have tried to write several times but could not. My heart still aches when I think of you and Jake. I always loved him, but never stood a chance. You simply batted your long eyelashes and looked up at him with your big blue eyes. Janet, please accept my sincere appology and find it in your heart to forgive me. I deeply regret my actions after you announced your engagement. I am sincerely sorry for all the grief I caused with my pouting and silence. I will write a long newsy letter in a few days. I now have two beaus who are constantly asking me out. Our little sisters are now sixteen and fourteen and have beaus as well. Congratulations. You two must be excited about having your first baby.

Mother worries about you being so far away from a doctor at this time.

Your sister, Abigail

I cupped my chin in my hands as my thoughts wandered. Finally, a name! Another question answered. Abigail was her sister. What was their last name? Was "Morgan" Janet's maiden name?

I picked up the diary to continue reading.

September 30, 1910

Jake brought home a small trunk from my family that contained an assortment of fabrics, baby clothes and household items that included my great grandmothers bronze candle stick holders and two large boxes of candles. What a delightful surprise.

Jake bought an oil lamp which makes a brighter light than a candle. I am keeping the candles for the times we are out of fuel for the lamp.

It becomes dark early now, and sometimes the only light is from the fireplace. I feel closed in with the tall trees surrounding the cabin. There are days when the sky is the colour of a dove, and the clouds are so close that I feel like I can reach up and touch them.

Jake built a dome-shaped fireplace near the step, with a shelf that holds three loaves of bread. He starts a fire early in the morning, which quickly heats up the oven. My bread is much better now.

I have memorized the letters from my little sisters full of their school activities and can see them when I close my eyes. They are growing up so quickly.

The days are lonely but busy. The baby kicks all night—at least, it feels that way. As soon as I lie down, the baby starts thrasing around. It feels like he or she is wearing army boots.

The forest is a pleasing mixture of gold, red, green and yellow against the backdrop of the tall evergreen trees. The trees sounded like a bird hotel this morning. Soon they will be gone, and all will be silent.

I made a few notes in my notebook and put everything back in the drawer. I wandered into the kitchen and helped Gramma make cookies, forgetting about J. D.—whom I now know is Janet.

When I opened the oven door to take out the last tray of chocolate chip cookies, a blast of hot steamy air hit me in the face. I had just set the tray on top of the stove when Megan burst into the room, stomping her feet. Her cheeks were rosy like apples, and she looked like Frosty the Snowman.

"Lassie, you're making a mess all over my clean floor." Gramma handed Megan a mop. "Clean up that snow."

"Do you want some hot chocolate and cookies?" I arranged chocolate chip cookies on a plate.

"I would love some. Wait till you hear the news," Megan cleaned up the snow and hung up her snowsuit.

"What's up?" I took two green mugs out of the cupboard beside the sink.

"Father met Austin and Kyle Cross. They are mischievous, and a bit spoiled." Megan said.

"They won't get away with much at school." I poured hot chocolate into the mugs.

"They got into trouble at the store. Dan watched them swipe candy while Father stocked shelves," Megan slid onto the bench behind the oak table.

"That took a lot of nerve." Steam twirled as it rose from the mugs as I filled them.

"Father made Kyle and Austin stock the storeroom shelves," Megan cupped her hands around the warm mug letting the warmth seep through her fingers.

"What do they look like?" I asked.

Megan took a sip before saying, "They have curly black hair and dark blue eyes with long lashes that sweep down to their chubby cheeks."

I cradled my warm mug in my hands. "That's not fair."

"No, it's not." Megan paused to take a bite of cookie. "Mr. Anderson is planning on giving everyone a sleigh ride home after school Monday."

"Sounds like fun." I took a bite out of my cookie. "Won't it be cold?"

"Mr. Anderson has fur rugs and blankets in the sleigh so it should be cozy," Megan pushed her mug away. "Mother had said not to be too long, so I'd better get going. See you later."

After Megan left, I strolled into the living room. My thoughts drifted to Father. I had almost started talking to him the other day but caught myself just in time.

Pumpkin padded over to the fireplace and turned around in circles before he settled in front of the hearth.

***

It had been a fun-filled weekend and Monday morning came quickly. The sound of shuffling feet filled the classroom as we made our way to our desks.

The only sound was the scraping of pencils as we copied our assignment from the blackboard. Ten minutes later, Austin and Kyle strolled in. They stood by the door, looking around the room, giggling and giving each other sly looks.

"Why are you late?" Miss Grayson paused in the instruction she was giving the grade ones.

The twins shrugged. "Just because." They said almost simultaneously.

"Take your seats. Kyle, beside Miranda. Austin, beside Bess." Miss Grayson passed them textbooks. "Assignments are written on the blackboard."

Austin fidgeted with his papers and books. He leaned sideways and whispered to me, "Help me with the assignment. It will be worth your while."

I glanced at him, shook my head and tried to ignore him. I turned my back so he could not copy my work.

He poked me. "What is the matter, cat got your tongue? Can't you talk?"

"Quit it. Quit trying to copy my work and do your own." I turned and glared at him.

The teacher crossed her arms across her chest. "Enough."

Austin brushed his hand against his arithmetic book, knocking it on the floor with a bang while he peeked over my shoulder. "Oops. Sorry, teach."

"Pickup your book and continue with your assignment."

"My hand slipped," he said with a smirk.

"Stand in the corner. You can catch up at recess."

***

After recess, desks banged as we prepared to do our assignments. Austin and Kyle made faces at Megan and me and fidgeted with their books.

"Psst, Bess. Help with my spelling," Austin said.

My muscles tightened, and I squared my shoulders. "No. Do your own."

"Hey, come on. Don't be so stuck up." Austin tugged my braid.

I glared at him and lifted my chin. "Quit trying to cheat and do your work."

"Austin, sit on the stool in the corner for the rest of the morning." Miss Grayson paused in the instruction she was giving the grade two students.

I had just finished my assignment when Miss Grayson dismissed us for lunch, and we gathered in small groups.

"What do you do around here for fun?" Austin took a sandwich out of his Roy Rogers lunch pail.

"Some of us are playing cowboys and Indians. Do you want to join us?" Jeff opened his thermos. "I have chores and homework after school."

***

The rest of the day went without further incidents because Miss Grayson made Austin sit by himself. Paper rustled, and pencils scraped as we bent over our desks doing assignments.

Before Miss Grayson dismissed us for the day, she stood in front of the blackboard. "Any volunteers to sweep the basement?"

Dan, Jeff and a couple of the other boys put their hands up.

"Good." Miss Grayson wrote their names on the blackboard. "Anyone else?"

Austin and Kyle looked at each other and snickered. "Ask the janitor," Austin said.

"Good two more volunteers," Miss Grayson wrote Kyle and Austin's names on the board. "Everyone is dismissed. See you in the morning."

Kyle narrowed his eyes. "Hey! I didn't volunteer."

Austin snorted. "That's the janitor's job."

"No more discussion. Everyone dismissed."

Desks slammed when we put our books away. The wooden floor creaked as we made our way to the cloakrooms. Miss Grayson smiled as she stood at the doorway helping the younger students with scarves, mittens, and hats. "Have a good evening."

Our footsteps crunched in the snow, and our breath looked like smoke as we hurried to the sleigh.

"I want to ride up front," Austin squished ahead of Jeff.

"I want to ride in front, too," Kyle pushed Megan out of the way.

"Get in the back with the other boys unless you want to walk. Girls up front," Mr. Anderson said in his deep baritone voice. "Is everyone in? Let's go."

Mr. Anderson drove the Clydesdales along at a slow and steady pace. The air was cold and crisp, but it was warm and cozy snuggled in rugs and quilts. We rode along in silence, listening to the sleigh bells and crunch of the horses' hoofs, as we passed through snowbanks that reached toward the sky and formed tunnels. Heavy snow pulled the tree branches down until they created arches. The edges of our scarves turned white with frosty crystals. The sunlight glittered on the snow making it hard on the eyes if you looked in one direction too long.

***

Later that afternoon, I took out Janet's diary instead of doing homework.

October 5, 1910

Jake carved an oak log to make a cradle. I made a blue ticking cover for the mattress that Jake filled with corn husks. And I made flannel blankets out of the fabric left in the trunk. Mother sent soft, warm baby blankets and tiny little nighties. My sisters knitted little green and yellow sweaters and bonnets. Our wee one will be warm and cozy.

Mrs. Knight, neighbour, and midwife, has been over a few times. She has helped in numerous births and will stay with us when my time is closer.

I rubbed my eyes and put the diary down. The writing was hard to read, and my eyelids felt heavy. I rested my head on the desk for a second.

I found myself inside the cabin watching Janet rocking the baby while Jake sat with his daughter on his knee. She was giggling as Jake bounced a teddy bear in his large hand. Janet was telling him something. What is she saying?

The door was open. Behind the door was a trunk, with suitcases on top. Dishes spilled out of crates with mounds of bedding on the chairs. Janet was pale and thin. A girl came through the open door with a couple of pails of water. Who is that? Their voices blended in with other sounds.

I awoke with a start when Pumpkin stretched up against my leg, purring. Why could I see the people as plain as day but could not hear the conversation? I shook my head in disbelief and put the diary away before heading toward the kitchen.

When I returned, I set my snack on my desk and cleared off the left side and took out my paint-by-numbers. As I concentrated on matching the numbers and colours, I managed to put Jake and Janet out of my mind for the rest of the evening. We were going to learn how to do a real painting when Miss Prate started our art class.

***

The rest of the week went smoothly, without any disruptions from Kyle and Austin. They were starting to fit in a little bit. We waited for our art lesson and had just finished our assignments Friday afternoon when Miss Prate arrived with a wicker basket full of art supplies.

The twins rushed forward. "Can we pass things out?"

"Hand out the drawing paper and pencils. Then take your seats," Miss Grayson said.

"The first task is to draw something on your paper," Miss Prate walked up and down the aisles. "Sketch anything you like."

The clock ticked and pencils tapped on desks as we concentrated on our sketches. Then Austin and Kyle put their hands up.

"Yes, boys?" Miss Grayson said.

"Look at our drawings," Kyle and Austin said almost simultaneously.

Miss Prate walked down the aisle, her heels clicking on the wooden floor. "They are excellent; you have talent. Don't waste it."

"Which one do you like best? My car?" Austin asked.

"Do you like my sketch?" Kyle asked as he held up a drawing of Miss Grayson.

"They're both good," Miss Prate said.

"Let's hang them up," Miss Grayson said with a smile.

"I have set up a still life of books, a vase, and apples on the desk," Miss Prate said. "That is what you will draw next. We will display your work for a week, and then you can take them home."

Everyone was silent—even Kyle and Austin—as we drew the objects as best we could. The room was so quiet you could have heard a pin drop.

The afternoon went quickly, and Miss Grayson said, "Time to clean up."

"Next week, everyone will paint a snow scene. Pay attention to how the sky meets the ground. That is your horizon line," Miss Prate collected the drawings.

The room sounded like a busy beehive as we made our way to the cloakrooms. My breath looked like smoke when Megan and I went out into the frosty air toward Aunt Anna's car.

***

Later that afternoon, I dumped my book bag on my bed while Pumpkin leaped onto the window seat and scratched at his reflection in the window. I pulled out the white chair in front of my desk. I cupped my chin in my hand as my thoughts wandered. My sketches did not resemble the objects that were on Miss Grayson's desk. Apparently, I do not have much art talent. Some of the things looked like blobs.

I sighed as I opened the desk drawer. My thoughts returned to the old cabin and the things I had learned about its previous occupants. I took the old diary out and laid it on the desk and opened it to the last entry I had read. I took one look at the dainty writing and thought about all the unanswered questions. Shaking my head, I put the diary back in the drawer unread and picked up my white diary and silver pen.

November 1954

Dear Diary,

It has been busy, and I have not had time to write my thoughts down. Things have been interesting at school. Miss Grayson is at her wits' end and does not know what to do with Kyle and Austin.

Mother bought me new skirts, blouses and new novels at The Next to New Consignment store. She says I am growing like a weed. I especially like the red sweater and the navy cardigan.

I was thinking of Father again this morning, and I know Mother was, too. It's Father's birthday, which makes it twice as difficult.

Uncle Joe is making good progress with his restoration project. He is past the messy, dusty stage. He restored the old logs, and each one is at least three feet high. It is hard to imagine that was Jake and Janet's living space—bedroom, living room and kitchen. Uncle Joe found the hidden latch for the door and will fix it in the spring when he is doing outside work.

I still have not found out what Jake and Janet's last name was. If I knew, it would be easier to track them down. So far, no one has ever heard of them.

Pat was over to fix the hinge on the back door and a few other things. He enjoys talking about what I am finding in the old diaries.

Chapter 9 Megan Helps with Research

As I put sandwiches on a silver tray, I glanced at the small framed sketch hanging by the window. With Miss Prate's help, my artwork had improved over the last couple of weeks. A knock on the door brought me out of my daydream.

"Goodness. They're early," Gramma took off her apron and placed the trays in the refrigerator.

I answered the door. "Good morning! Come in." Miss Prate wore blue coveralls and a plaid cotton shirt with her grey braids wrapped on the top of her head.

"I know I'm a bit early, but I had some things that might help with your research and a quilt top to show your Gramma before the others get here." She set the quilt on the table.

"Let me help you bring everything inside." I handed Gramma the last tray of sandwiches before I grabbed my parka.

"There are several boxes of old newspapers and ledgers from the sawmill office," Miss Prate said as she followed me outside. "All the records and news are in them."

We made a couple of trips to Miss Prate's Jeep and put the last box in a pile by the kitchen doorway. "Thank you. Megan is coming later, and I will ask her to help go through the newspapers."

"Show us your quilt top," Gramma said.

The clock ticked and Pumpkin purred as he rubbed against my leg while Miss Prate unfolded the fabric and spread it on the table. My pulse quickened as I gazed at the pioneer village embroidered on pale green fabric. Log cabins were nestled in the dense forest. "Is that the saloon? What are those other buildings?" I asked, pointing. "Would that be Jake and Janet's cabin? It's the last one, and then trees. The landscape has changed from what it used to be."

"It has changed over the years. I used an old map and notes that were in Father's office for a reference." Miss Prate pointed to the different buildings. "There's the general store, blacksmith shop and stable."

"It will be a treasure," Gramma said. "What colour do you want to use for a border?"

"Navy blue or forest green," Miss Prate said. "It's a wedding present for Miss Grayson."

"Use forest green," Gramma answered.

"Oh, she'll love it," I helped fold it. "Do you remember much about the village and the little cabin?"

"I just heard bits and pieces of stories that had been passed down through the generations," Miss Prate answered. "From what I heard, it was a rough village. The population consisted mostly of woodchoppers who spent their evenings and free time in the saloon. They ate and cashed their paycheques there. Of course, a lot of whisky went down with their meals."

"According to your quilt, the saloon was close to where the school is now," I said.

"Yes, it would have been, wouldn't it?" Miss Prate said. "Dense forest surrounded the buildings and no park. Indians and pioneers made narrow winding trails—like the ones near the sawmill."

"It's hard to imagine," I said. "Everything except the cabin was close to the river."

"The pioneers depended on the river for water, transportation, and food. An abundance of fish filled the river. Did you notice the little creek behind the cabin?" Miss Prate set the folded quilt aside. "Will Miss Grayson be here today? The quilt has to be a surprise."

"Yes, she said she would drop in after lunch," Gramma picked up the quilt top. "We are doing a quilt for Ava today, and the quilting frame is set up in the living room. I'll take this up to my sitting room…be right back."

My mind drifted as Gramma and Miss Prate visited while they waited for the rest of the women to come. They talked about current events and nothing else about the town back in 1908 or beyond.

It was boring listening to their everyday gossip, so I started to take the boxes to my room and stacked them beside my bed and desk. I took out the bundle of letters and picked up the first one. I opened the delicate page and smoothed out the deep creases.

To my Dearest Janet,

I write a few lines to say I am well, thank god. I was plesased to get your last letter. It brought joy to my heart that youse were making travelling arrangements for your journey west. I was glad to hear youse would have travelling companions.

A couple of men from the mill helped build this sturdy cabin in the middle of a meadow with a babbling brook behind which will provide lots of water until I can dig a well. The meadow is full of wildflowers and wild strawberries and other fruit. I cleared a small space nearby for a vegetable garden. The cabin consists of one large room with a table underneath the window. The stone fireplace takes up one wall and is large enough to walk in.

There have been a couple of cold days but is milder again today. The winter has been lovely so far, just snow enough for sleighing and the weather has been so mild most of the time. I made shelves for your books. Bring as many as youse want. The mill isn't as busy now, but there is lots of work in the bush. Must go now. I look forward to the New Year and the day when youse join me. I have enclosed a list of items youse should bring along.

Your loving, affectionate husband,

Jake

I folded the letter. What was the last name? Were there answers in the stack of newspapers or the boxes of ledgers and papers? I glanced at the clock on the nightstand and realized Megan would be arriving soon. I put everything away in the desk drawer and headed down the hallway with Pumpkin strutting behind.

I was putting sandwiches on a plate when Megan burst into the kitchen. "I got my puppy yesterday. You'll have to see him soon! He is copper-coloured, with large adorable brown eyes. I haven't decided on a name yet, but he is such a little scamp and rascal."

"Help me set the lunch trays up for the ladies. Miss Prate brought over boxes of old newspapers and ledgers that were in her father's office," I picked up a tray of sandwiches. "We're allowed to have lunch in my bedroom today."

"I'd love to help," Megan picked up a silver tray and followed me into the living room, which sounded like a busy beehive. Everyone paused when we arrived with plates of dainty sandwiches, cookies, and tarts that we set on a small round table by the window. Chairs held up the colourful quilt stretched on a wooden frame. The furniture had been pushed back to accommodate the large quilt. As soon as we set the sandwich trays and large silver teapot on the table—for everyone to help themselves—we continued down the hallway to my room with our refreshments.

Megan and I sat cross-legged on the double bed. "Isn't it exciting about Miss Grayson's engagement? She has been teaching here for five years."

Pumpkin bumped my hand until I started to pet him. "I am going to miss Miss Grayson."

"What about the old cabin? How's the research going?" Megan sprawled across the bed on her stomach.

"Miss Prate brought over boxes of old newspapers and ledgers. There might be more information in them," I said. "Let's eat first."

"Good. I'm starving," Megan stretched and sat up. "Everything looks scrumptious. Fancy, too, with the crusts cut off." She helped herself to an egg salad sandwich. "Father is making good progress with the cabin. He is amazed at how well it has held together." She paused to take a bite.

We ate in silence while Pumpkin kneaded a pillow in front of the bookcase. I wiped crumbs off my blue blouse onto my rose patterned plate. "There are still a lot of questions."

Megan set her plate on the nightstand, "Where do you want to start?"

"The newspapers." I hopped off the bed and picked up the stack from the early 1900's.

The ladies' voices, which carried down the hallway, distracted me. After a few minutes, I got up and closed my door. We worked silently, and paper rustled as we turned the pages. Pumpkin tried to get our attention by batting the paper. Megan's eyes sparkled when she looked up. "Listen to this. It's an interesting article in December 29th edition of the Times."

Fateful Fire

Around midnight on December 28, a fire started in the saloon. The loggers had received their paycheques. They ate and drank whisky all night. After midnight, the fire bells rang, rousing everyone within a couple miles' radius. All the locals battled the blaze well into the morning. They were not able to save the saloon, and the fire spread into the forest. Many trees burned down, but snow fell at dawn, saving the surrounding businesses and cabins. Several loggers perished in the blaze. Most of the dance hall women escaped with only the clothes on their backs. Some folks are against the idea of having saloon dancers

67

and do not want the saloon rebuilt. More families are in the area now, and they want a school and a church.

"How awful. Those people in the saloon would never have known what was happening until it was too late." I looked up from the papers on my lap. "Nothing here."

"I have to go home and check on my puppy. Mother and Father are not home," Megan set the newspaper on the desk. "I found items that would go with our social studies. Nothing about the cabin though."

I walked down the hallway with her. "I will look some more after supper. I hope to find their last name. I found interesting things in the diaries and old letters. Janet and Jake loved each other very much. It is quite the love story. She was from a wealthy family and fell in love with a man who was below her class."

The rest of the day was busy, and I did not have time to go back to the research. Gramma wanted me to help clean up after the women left. We took the completed quilt off the frame and folded it before putting it in Gramma's sitting room.

"We will have another quilting party in a month to do Miss Prate's quilt. It will be a treasure. She is going to buy some fabric for the backing and border. There is still enough batting left," Gramma took the sandwiches off the ornate silver tray.

"I still haven't found Janet and Jake's last name. The old newspapers contained many interesting articles especially the one about the saloon burning down," I handed Gramma the silver tea service. "Miss Grayson wants everyone to find interesting stories about the town, past or present."

"How interesting," Gramma said. "Sounds like an item for your social studies."

"Yes, I'll write a report for my assignment."

"Good idea," Gramma put the platters in the cupboard.

***

Pumpkin curled up on my lap, purring, a few days later while I did my homework. "There. Finished." My thoughts drifted to the things I'd learned about Janet and Jake. I furrowed my brow as I rested my chin in my hands. What was their last name?

I opened the desk drawer and took out my diary and pen.

November 1954

Dear Diary,

The days are busy with school, homework and by the time I go to bed, I fall asleep as soon as my head hits the pillow. Last night I stayed up late finishing a book that Pat had loaned me. I had a flashlight under the covers so no one would know I was still awake. It was difficult to get up this morning.

We had a surprise visit from Mr. and Mrs. Mar, our old neighbours from Oak River. Gramma and Mrs. Mar exchanged old recipes that were mostly in their heads. They are both old-fashioned cooks who use a pinch of this and that. How they can keep everything straight in their minds is a mystery.

Austin and Kyle are still getting into all kinds of mischief in school and out. Of course, Jeff is happy about not being the only boy in our class. Some of the other boys used to tease him about it when Miss Grayson could not hear or see them. None of us are model students because we often whisper to one another or pass an occasional note. But we always get our assignments done in class to avoid getting extra homework.

Chapter 10 A Discovery

A week later, the classroom was a buzz of activity as we prepared for the day. I copied down assignments from the blackboard while Austin doodled in his notebook. He held it up to show me. "What do you think of my drawing of your cat? You can have it."

"It looks natural. I would love to have it. Thank you." I glanced at Austin's notebook for a minute.

Miss Grayson stood in front of her desk. "Can I have everyone's attention? Your social studies papers were well done. A few were exceptional." The room was silent, other than the ticking of the clock as Miss Grayson walked up and down the aisle. "Bess did a lot of research, while Austin and Kyle used their imaginations, as did Jeff. Congratulations to everyone for their hard work."

"I like to imagine what it would have been like back in the days when the saloon was here. My buddies and I often use the foundation as a fort," Jeff's eyes sparkled.

"What is all the fuss about all the old stuff? The future sounds more interesting than the past," Kyle and Austin glanced at each other.

"Your accompanying sketches made your pieces interesting. Each of you presented different ideas," Miss Grayson said with a smile.

"The pioneers laid down the path for us to have the life we enjoy now." I raised my eyebrows as I glanced at Kyle and Austin.

Miss Grayson paused at Kyle's desk. "Where did you learn to sketch like that?"

"I don't know. Just always done it," Kyle answered.

"This is the sketch Kyle has been doing while we were talking." Miss Grayson held up a lifelike sketch of a fox. "It's very good, but please keep your sketching to your free time and art class. It isn't something to do in social studies."

"All right. I was still paying attention," Kyle said with a shrug.

The room was hushed for the rest of the afternoon as we worked on assignments. Miss Grayson helped the younger children. Even Austin and Kyle were on their best behaviour because we studied science and social studies, two of their favourite subjects.

The afternoon went quickly, and the room was filled with the racket of desks banging and rustling paper when we were dismissed.

After supper, I set my arithmetic aside to look through the stack of old letters. I picked up an envelope that contained a letter addressed to Mr. and Mrs. Jake Dale from Mr. and Mrs. L Dale. Could they be Jakes's parents?

Dear Jake and Janet,

We were pleased when we finally got your letter about the birth of your daughter. It was welcome news when you told us that Mrs. Knight, who could perform midwife duties, stayed until Janet was back on her feet again after the birth of your daughter. I am sure this was a relief to Janet's family, as well.

Your grandmother would have been pleased that you named your daughter after her. Rebecca is a pretty name.

I will write a longer letter later. I wanted to get this ready to go along with the little parcel we are sending the wee one.

All my love, Mother

P.S.

Hi Son,

Have you given any more thought about buying a little farm? Your mother and I would be able to back you on such a venture. Your job at the mill sounds good, but is it a good place for a young family? You mentioned, in one of your letters, that there are more families in the farming community. Please let us know what your plans are now that you are a parent yourself.

Father

My eyelids felt heavy, so I rested my head on my desk for a second.

I found myself walking up a narrow, neglected path toward the empty cabin. Nature was reclaiming the little garden, and the step was crumbling. I paused, looking around feeling puzzled. Had they been gone for a long time? A group of little boys was fishing by the creek.

The door swung on homemade hinges. Nail marks indicated where they had blankets hung to divide the bedroom area. The space was full of leaves, and other debris. I shuddered when I almost ran into a spider web. Sunlight peeked through the cracks in the closed unpainted shutters. A small table leaned against the wall under the window with broken chairs scattered around the room. A trunk with suitcases on top stood in the corner. The distant sound of a door opening and closing blended into my dream.

The sound of Pumpkin landing on the floor with a thump brought my mind back to the present. Was it just a dream, or did I go back in time for a brief second?

I picked up the diary again to read the last entries.

December 30, 1911

It is just about the end of another year. I can be thankful for all our good fortune. Our future holds many promises. Even with all the hard work, we are happy. In the evenings, when Rebecca is sleeping in her crib, Jake often sings or plays quietly on his ukulele. I wish I had my piano because I miss it so. But that is when I do my mending or make new clothes for our sweet baby girl. She is growing rapidly.

Jake is snoring, and Rebecca is sleeping soundly. I should be sleeping as well because tomorrow will be another busy day, but sleep eludes me tonight. Jake was thrilled when I told him we would be parents again. I am just starting to show.

I will now go back and record some of the events leading up to Rebecca's birth.

October had been warm and sunny. The trees were a mixture of red, gold and green. Birds gathered in large flocks, and I loved listening to their impromto concerts. That came to an abrupt halt near the end of the month.

The morning started warm, but by noon, purple clouds hung low in the sky. The wind picked up leaves and swirled them around in circles while the baby kicked violently. I had a mild backache but did not think too much about it because I was not due until nearly the middle of November. The wind rattled the door and shutters It was cozy near the fireplace, but when you walk away from the fire, the air has a chill to it.

I kept stirring stew in the big iron pot that hung from a hook over the fire. I put towels over five loaves of fresh bread. It is amazing that with just the two of us, how fast it can disappear! The fierce wind made it difficult to close the shutters. (There is not any glass in the window—just an oilcloth—which always made it feel gloomy inside.)

My backpain increased, and I worried that Jake wouldn't get home in time. The wind intensified, and snow swirled around the yard, and Jake still was not home. It was dark outside, making it feel like late at night instead of early afternoon. The only light was from the fireplace, so I lit one of my precious candles.

At that moment, Jake stumbled inside, looking like a snowman. Just behind him was Mrs. Knight. I was never so glad to see anyone in my life! The wind snatched the door out of Jake's hands, and he wrestled with it for a few minutes, but finally closed it. Mrs. Knight met Jake at the mill because she had a premonition. People around here always say she has second sight, which she got from her mother and grandmother. Lately, I've wanted my mother so badly. I long for her advice and counsel.

The storm intensified as my labour pains got closer togeather and Jake made a bed close to the fireplace. He paced the floor, almost wearing a path in the braided rug I had finished the day before.

Rebecca was born at midnight. A little red and wrinkled, but she had a healthy set of lungs because she sure did holler. She has grown rapidly since then.

Mrs. Knight stayed with us until I was well enough to get up and tend to household duties. One morning, Mr. Knight came to fetch her. He was getting lonely and found it difficult to manage their noisy household. He also missed her baking.

I closed the diary and made a few notes in my notebook before returning everything to the desk drawer. I looked up when Mother came into the room. "Why are you still up? It's time you went to bed, my dear."

"In a few minutes. I am sure glad for modern conveniences. Pioneers built this town, and even through all their hardships, kept going," I said with a yawn.

"Good night, dear, and sweet dreams," Mother said as she turned to leave.

"Can Megan, Miranda and Josie sleep over?" I asked.

"Of course. You need to think of other things besides Jake and Janet," Mother smile crinkled the edge of her eyes. "You are spending too much time on that and your studies. Have some fun for a change."

"Okay, Mother. It turns out Jake was a Dale. I would like to find out if they are related to Sadie," I said. "Can we visit Sadie and her father? Sadie had said he does genealogy research and might have records dating back to Jake and Janet's marriage."

"Yes, of course. I'll speak to Sadie in a few days," Mother said. "Now go to bed. We'll discuss it later."

I snuggled under the covers with a flashlight in hand with my diary and pen and started to write.

December 1954

Dear Diary,

We have been reviewing for our Christmas exams which doesn't leave much time for anything else. I will be glad when exams are over especially arithmetic which is my worst subject. There is a couple of new books laying on the window seat that I am longing to read but have to wait until after exams.

I finished my paint by numbers, and they are leaning on my bookshelves. I enjoyed painting them, and maybe one day I will learn to draw cats so I can paint Pumpkin.

Mrs. Snow loaned me a couple of books about the pioneers, and I have found interesting stories in them. It makes me appreciate the modern conveniences we have, but I am thankful they created this charming village.

Chapter 11 The End of the Old Diaries

After a couple of weeks of constant reviewing the dreaded Christmas, exams are over. The only cloud that falls over everything is getting our report cards when Miss Grayson has marked all the exams. I opened my desk drawer and took out Janet's old diary. There were only a couple of entries left. The rest of the pages were stuck together, and the writing so badly smudged it was impossible to read.

July 30, 1912

Rebecca is growing out of everything, and it is hard to keep up with my sewing. Thankfully, Mother and Mother Dale always send me packages with lots of warm clothes. I would not be able to keep up with the demand if they did not.

Since I last wrote, I have had a son—Jake's pride and joy. Jake carves toys for both of the children. I'm on my feet all day and only sit down when I am feeding Jake Junior. He is a sweet, cuddly baby. I don't seem to have enough energy to get all my work done. This time it was a more difficult delivery, and my recovery was longer.

Jake and I discussed getting someone to live with us and help with some of the household chores. One of Mrs. Knights daughters will move in. It will be nice to have the company during the day.

August 1912

Jake wanted to look at a nearby farm. It hadn't rained all week which made it a good time to take a buggy ride out to see the property. If it had rained the roads would have been slipperly with big mud puddles but with the favourable conditions Jake had to concentrate on keeping the buggy wheels out of the many potholes and the deep ruts from heavy wagons that pass through the area everyday. It was a cool evening with a nice breeze that helped keep the bugs away.

It is a pretty place surrounded by majestic trees on top of a hill. We could not go in the house because no one was home. The owner, a widower, does not want to continue farming. There is a two-story stone house with glass windows and a large clearing with a garden in the back. A log stable is just beyond the trees. There are five bedrooms upstairs and one bedroom on the main floor. It will feel like a palace after living in this little cabin!

I am pregnant again. Mrs. Knights daughter moved in and is delightful company. She does most of the heavy cleaning and getting water from the creek so I can get some badly needed rest.

Mother and Father Dale and my sister Abigail are coming for a visit. I look forward to seeing Abigail again. We will have much more space in the new house and will be easier to clean.

I squeezed the middle of my nose and wrinkled my brow as I focused on the smudged dainty writing. I closed the journal after leafing through the last blank pages. There hadn't been any more entries, but it sounded like she was looking forward to moving into a larger house. I took a few notes as I wrapped up my research.

Pumpkin jumped on my lap and bumped my hand. After I had given him a gentle hug, I turned my attention back to my studying.

***

The week had dragged by but it was finally Friday, and we waited anxiously for our report cards. There was the sound of rustling paper as Miss Grayson passed them out. "Everyone did well. Your hard work paid off."

My pulse quickened as I scanned the page, and then I let out a long breath. Megan had a wide grin when she turned around to give me a questioning look.

Miss Grayson paused in front of her desk. "Can I have everyone's attention?" As soon as the room was quiet, she said, "It's time to plan the Christmas concert."

Miss Grayson wrote the concert program on the blackboard. "We will do the Christmas story, a few plays, and recitals and sing carols."

The room was filled with the buzz of youthful voices as we talked about report cards and the upcoming concert.

***

Later that evening, I took my white diary out of the desk drawer.

December 1954

Dear Diary,

I am so glad that exams are over and I can relax a bit more. It is going to be fun rehearsing for our Christmas concert. Everyone is going to have a part in something.

79

Mother has been rearranging the living room. She will not tell me why but has a mysterious smile on her face. Something is up, but I do not know what. It is the time of year for secrets.

I was pleased when I got my marks back. They were between 70–80%. I was just a little behind Kyle and Austin. They seem to be able to get good marks without even trying. It just does not seem fair. I want to be a teacher like Father when I graduate.

Megan, Miranda, and Josie are going to have a sleepover on the weekend, and I am looking forward to it. Mother says I have been working too hard and should have a night of girl talk and fun. She is right.

My thoughts have been with my father the last few days because this will be the first Christmas without him.

Megan, Miranda, and Josie are going to help decorate the Christmas tree. I made paper ornaments, pom-poms and braided chains that are cat-proof because Pumpkin has never seen a Christmas tree before. He might think the ornaments are toys. Mother got ornaments at the second-hand store. She does not want to use any of the delicate glass ones. Father used to buy a new ornament every year. I think she just wants it to be a bit different.

Mother and I will visit Sadie Dale and her father soon. I have many unanswered questions, and I hope they can answer them.

Chapter 12 The Sleepover

I strung popcorn and cranberries onto strings to make garlands for the Christmas tree. The late afternoon sunlight made the frosty windows sparkle. My fingers worked rapidly while my mind wandered. I had just finished the tree garlands when Megan, Miranda, and Josie arrived.

"Hey! You started without us," Josie picked up a string of popcorn and cranberries. "You made a lot."

"Let's decorate the tree," I started to clean up. "Any leftovers will go on the outside trees and in the birdfeeder."

Megan, Miranda, Josie and I giggled as we strung the popcorn on the Scotch pine. Pumpkin sat nearby, wiggling his bum as he got ready to pounce on the strings of popcorn.

"Not for you," Miranda took one end of a string out of his paws.

Pumpkin ducked under the lower branches and peeked out waiting for his opportunity to snatch one of the decorations that dangled above his nose. He started to swat them gently until he worked one loose and dashed across the room with an ornament in his mouth.

"Come back with that!" Megan chased Pumpkin down the hallway. After a few minutes, she put the red and gold ball back onto the tree. "Let's put the star on top. Then we are done."

"It looks good," Josie said. "Bess, did you ever find out why your mother has been rearranging the furniture?"

"No, but Pat has been helping her move the heavy pieces. Whatever it is, Gramma is in on it. They give each other funny looks every once in a while." I set the empty ornament box to one side.

"Where is the wingback chair from the corner? It used to be beside the window," Miranda's brow wrinkled as she looked around the room.

"Well, beats me." I took a silver bell out of Pumpkin's paws. "Gramma made sandwiches for us. Let's eat and then put on pyjamas."

I sat cross-legged on the golden oak sleigh bed in yellow flannel pyjamas, brushing my hair. Josie plumped up pillows as she settled on the window seat with a newspaper. Miranda was in the middle of the floor with Pumpkin curled up on her lap, while Megan sat cross-legged leaning against the window seat.

Pumpkin padded toward the bed and jumped up, landing on the open newspaper. "You're not much help," I said, pushing the orange cat to the side. Pumpkin purred and kneaded the patchwork quilt.

We had been visiting and looking through the old newspapers and movie magazines for half an hour when Josie looked up. Her finger marking an item. "Remember that fire Bess told us about in social studies? The one that almost burned the town down. Listen to this."

Town Saved by Snowstorm

The fire destroyed the saloon and trees for miles around. The blacksmith shop and the stable were soon lost and the men barely got the horses out in time. Two men staggered out of the stable wondering what was happening. There are no casualties after all.

Dark clouds covered the moon, but it was bright as day as the flames leaped high into the sky. In the middle of the night, it started to snow, and the wind picked up. At that time, we thought the general store was a goner. Fortunately, the snow increased and drifts of snow soon formed. Within an hour, the snow had put out the fire—other than a few hot spots, where it smouldered.

The storm increased during the night, covering the burned buildings, while tree skeletons poked out through the blanket of snow. The town council is surveying the area for a new location for some of the buildings away from the charred remains. The fire missed the general store and a couple of other buildings which were further away.

Pumpkin snuggled on my lap, purring, as I listened to Josie. "Jeff had said the foundations of the blacksmith shop and saloon are near the edge of the schoolyard."

"Do you think there is any of Gramma's chocolate cake left?" Megan put the newspapers back in the box. "Do you think you could keep the newspapers for awhile. Some of the articles would tie in with our social studies."

"Yes, there is half a cake left." I put my hairbrush on the night stand and hopped off the bed landing with a thud. "Good idea."

We sat in the middle of the floor eating cake and drinking milk. Miranda twirled a strand of hair around her little finger. "It will feel strange sharing Mother with Tom after they get married."

"I thought you liked him." I played with the crumbs on my green plate.

"Yes, I like him as a friend, but I have never had a father." Miranda picked up her blue glass and had a sip of milk.

"Your mother looks happy." Josie pushed her hair out of her eyes.

"Yes, but there is too much kissing and hugging going on when they think I'm not looking. Ugh." Miranda set her glass and plate on the window seat and crawled into her sleeping bag.

"Do you remember your father?" Megan wiped the milk moustache off with her cloth napkin.

"Just from pictures. I was just a baby when he passed away." Miranda fluffed up her pillow. "Are you done with the old diaries and your research."

"Yes. Mother and I are going to visit Sadie and her father. It turns out Jake and Janet's last name was Dale. Morgan was her maiden name. It is no wonder no one had ever heard of Abigail Morgan." I put the plates and glasses on the window seat before snuggling into my sleeping bag.

***

It had been a busy week and Mother, and I were going to visit Sadie and her father. I put my notebook away after jotting down a few notes before taking out my diary.

December 1955

Dear Diary,

It has been a while since I wrote down my thoughts, which sometimes get jumbled up in my mind. I always feel relieved when I write them down.

I have come to the end of my research into the log cabin that is in Uncle Joe's house. There was a deep love between Jake and Janet that withstood all their hardships.

Our Christmas concert went well. Kyle and Austin painted all the backdrops for the plays. Mother's big surprise was a television.

Megan and I used to watch the televisions at the store when we lived in the city. Father had planned on buying one if my marks improved.

School is out until after New Year's. Christmas was good but different. It was just Mother, Gramma, Uncle Joe, Aunt Anna and Megan.

The garden looks pretty tonight in the moonlight. A heavy blanket of snow weighs down the bushes and trees. It looks magical, with the appearance of little tunnels where the tree branches almost touch the ground. Popcorn garlands on the evergreen trees sparkle in the moonlight. Our snowmen are having a picnic around the wooden table with mounds of snow on top. There have been several light snowfalls, but nothing like the one we had in October. It has been very cold.

We had several sleigh rides in Mr. Anderson's sleigh. It is such fun. The sleigh bells echoed in the frosty air.

Chapter 13 Visiting the Dales

I sat at the kitchen table watching Gramma punch down bread dough with my notebook in front of me. I was waiting for Mother because we were going to the Dale farm. Hopefully, they would be related to Jake and Janet.

Mother entered the kitchen. "Are you ready?"

"Yes," I answered, standing up.

Our feet crunched on the hard-packed snow as we walked to the car. "How far is it to the Dale farm?"

"A mile and half north of town," Mother answered.

We drove through high snowdrifts that formed a tunnel, each lost in our thoughts. The only sounds were the hum of the motor and the crunch of the tires. I gazed around as we drove down the road.

Mother turned onto a long twisting lane. Her hands gripped the steering wheel as she tried to keep the tires out of the deep ruts until the lane widened and the farmyard came into view. Mother parked in front of a two-story stone house.

I opened the car door. "That red barn has an unusual design, with the ramp going up to the loft. I wonder what all the other little buildings are for?"

"Possibly to store farm equipment," Mother and I walked single file along the narrow path in the waist-high snow. My breath was frosty, and soon my scarf was stiff and white. The crunching of our feet rang in the crisp, clear air.

The doorbell chimes echoed through the house, followed by the sound of footsteps. A petite woman in a pale blue dress and white sweater greeted us. "Come in out of the cold," Sadie said in a soprano voice. "Father is waiting in the parlour."

Mother and I followed Sadie into a cozy room just off the kitchen. Mr. Dale was relaxing in a white wingback chair in front of the crackling fire in a huge stone fireplace. He was a round jolly man with a shiny bald head and a long white beard with a walrus moustache. Family portraits and framed photos covered the large oak mantel. A variety of books and antique ceramics filled two walls of bookcases.

"Father, this is Bess and her mother, Mrs. Silver." Sadie paused near the fireplace. "Excuse me while I prepare refreshments. Be right back."

"Glad to make your acquaintance," Mr. Dale folded his newspaper. "Sadie told me that you found old diaries, a trunk, and suitcases in the old cabin in your friend's modern cabin."

"Yes, I did. The diary had the initials J.D. embroidered on the cover and name 'Abigail Morgan' was on a scrap of paper." I gazed around the room that had an antique feel.

"It is a story I had heard all my life." Mr. Dale said in a soft voice. "Come, have a seat. I believe Sadie made tea. Here she comes now."

Sadie set a tray on the round table. "I hope everyone likes mint tea."

"Oh, I have never had any before," I accepted the dainty cup and saucer. I looked at the tiny roses as I watched the steam twirl in the air. I inhaled the scent of mint before taking a sip. "Yummy."

Sadie passed out dainty cookies. "Did you finish reading the diaries yet?"

"Yes. I didn't find out the last name until recently. I found a letter addressed to Mr. and Mrs. Jake Dale in a bundle of letters." I picked up a peanut butter cookie from the rose patterned plate.

"Take a look at those photos on the fireplace mantel. Those are our ancestors," Mr. Dale said. "All the family names are carved in the stones used to build the fireplace."

"Oh, look! Jake, Janet and the babies' names," I ran my hand over the rough stones. "There is Abigail's name as well."

"Yes, Jake and Janet were my third great-grandparents," Mr. Dale answered as he set his teacup down. "Both Janet and Abigail fell in love with Jake. He was a handsome, charming fellow who liked the ladies. Well, in the end, Jake chose Janet. Poor Abigail never stood a chance," Mr. Dale said.

"Why did they leave Janet's things behind?" I looked through the framed photographs. "The trunk and suitcases were filled with books, dresses, dainty embroidery and other items."

"Janet started another diary after they moved here, that said some of their things disappeared during the move. No one knew what happened. Janet had saved books for their children and was disappointed that they disappeared along with her other treasures. A sawmill worker who was helping them move was supposed to go back for the remainder, but he simply disappeared. He was never heard from again." Mr. Dale paused to take a sip of tea. "Janet was pregnant when they moved. There was a young girl who lived with them at that time and Abigail, her sister, came and helped with the children. Janet passed away when the baby was a year old."

"How sad. I was hoping for a better outcome." I set the dainty cup down on the round mahogany table. "Do you want everything we found?"

"Thank you for finding everything, and yes, I can come get them. I am in town every day," Sadie set her teacup on the silver tray. "Would you like to keep the trunk? You can put your treasures in it."

"Thank you," I turned my attention back to the fireplace mantel and the portraits. While the adults visited, my thoughts wandered.

The sound of Mother's voice, when she said it was time to go, brought my mind back to the present.

***

A couple of days later I packed the items from the trunk, including the old diary and journals. Miss Prate picked up the old ledgers and newspapers, and everything else returned to Mr. Dale and Sara. My room looked empty now—Gramma could not complain about the mess anymore. Christmas holidays are rapidly drawing to a close. School would start on Monday. It would be fun catching up with what everyone else was doing over the holidays. When I talked to Miss Prate, she told me that she would give the old newspapers to Miss Grayson for awhile to help with our social studies.

January 1, 1955,

Dear Diary,

It is the beginning of a new year, and I look forward to all kinds of adventures in the future. I haven't taken the time to write my thoughts down. It is time to write about events before everything slips my mind. Half of the year is over, and I look forward to what the rest of the school year will hold.

Josie told us we would have singing classes Friday afternoons during the last class. Mrs. Hub has a piano that she will donate to the school because her fingers are too stiff with arthritis to play. It sounds like it will be fun.

We still have Miss Grayson for six months and then she will be getting married. She isn't returning to teach at our school but will be going on a long European honey- moon.

I would never have believed I would fit in at Pineview school at first, but I have enjoyed it immensely. There hasn't been a dull moment since Kyle and Austin came to our school. There is a fierce competition between all the grade five students. All of our marks are in the 80's and 90's.

I am relieved to put Janet and Jake's story to rest. Strange things happen to me when I get thrown into solving a mystery for some reason or other. It sounds like it's an inherited trait which can be creepy and unsettling.

The End.

Books by M E Hembroff

Bess's Magical Garden

The sun streamed in the window and illuminated the ivy wallpaper. Bess looked around and felt bewildered until she remembered that she was in their new home in Pineview. After she was fully awake, she realized that the room looked different in the daylight. The streetlights were on when they had arrived the night before. She looked out the bay window and noticed the snow-white apple blossoms. So that was the fragrance she had smelt.

Bess's thoughts drifted back to the day she had collapsed in ballet class. An ambulance had rushed her to the hospital, where her parents met her. After several tests the doctors told them that she had a mild case of polio. She ended up spending many months in the hospital undergoing treatment and physical therapy before she was ready to go home. She had worked hard, but she still had to wear a brace and use a crutch.

Her thoughts were interrupted when Mother breezed into the room. "Rise and shine."

"Don't want to," Bess grumbled, as she brushed some tousled hair out of her eyes.

Mother smiled. "It's a warm sunny day. Let's have breakfast in the garden. "The air was filled with the scent of jasmine as she walked past. Mother took clean clothes out of the open suitcase on the window seat.

Bess rubbed the sleep out of her eyes. "Would rather eat here," she said. Didn't Mother know how difficult it was to walk that far? Megan, her cousin and best friend, had always dropped in before school, so they could eat breakfast together. Megan had lived in the apartment across the hall. Bess had stayed at Megan's last weekend, while Mother and Uncle Joe moved the furniture. Megan beat her at snakes and ladders and checkers several times. The fun filled weekend ended too soon, and her new life suddenly began. She and her mother had left the city early Monday morning and arrived at their Pineview home late last night.

It wasn't fair that Mother had wanted to move. The doctors had told Mother that Bess needed fresh air and light exercise and not to lie around the apartment all day.

"Get up and get dressed," Mother said firmly. "There will be all kinds of fun things to do this summer. Would you like to decorate your room?"

"What's the point? There isn't anything to do without Megan," Bess grumbled, rubbing the sleep from her eyes.

"There is a path near the patio door that leads into a sheltered garden. See you there shortly," Mother answered.

Bess reluctantly got out of bed. After tucking her crutch under her arm, she hobbled across the room to look at the clothes that Mother had laid out. Why did Mother want her to dress up? Weren't her everyday clothes good enough? As Bess tried to decide whether to wear the skirt or a pair of slacks, her thoughts drifted to that day six months ago when they'd received the news about the car crash that took Father away forever. Bess had waited at the hospital with Mother, because she had been released that same afternoon to continue therapy as an outpatient. She and her mother had received the news that someone had sped through a green light and rammed into the driver's side of the car, killing Father instantly.

Bess proceeded down the hallway to the patio door and hobbled down the path. She stopped and looked around in amazement. For a brief second, she thought that she saw an archway covered with orange flowers that lead into a colourful garden…but it was gone in an instant. Instead, an arch covered in tangled vines with a broken gate swung on its hinges. The space was overgrown with weeds and surrounded by a crumbling stone wall. A tangle of weeds almost hid the stepping stones. She proceeded to the stone bench in the middle of the yard. Not until Mother arranged a tray with an assortment of muffins and fruit did Bess realize how hungry she was.

Voices of Yesterday – Coming Soon

The North wind lashed at the Victorian Manor this day in late May 2013. The straight rows of poplars along the driveway swayed back and forth as the wind howled. Rain came down in sheets and formed streams where there wasn't any before.

Kate Hill closed her laptop and stared through the gap in the green drapes. Kate shuttered as she thought about the fire that killed families and destroyed a part of Riverdale, near the railway station, in the spring of 1946. One of her classmates gave her a copy of an obituary of members of the McCoy family. Gran never talked about this. I wonder why? The sound of Mom's voice brought her back to the present.

Kate turned to face her mom and looked around the room. It had once served as a formal parlour but now it was a cozy library with book shelves on either side of the brick fireplace. Mom had furnished the room when we'd moved here five years ago. Two wing chairs flanked the fireplace with a round mahogany table beside each.

Kate's Mom took off her gold rimmed glasses and set her red pen on the unmarked papers on the mahogany table. "How's your research for the Franklin Manor history coming?"

"Not good. There are too many gaps. Our history teacher has given the class an extension because everyone is having problems with research. The assignment is due in a week." Kate gazed at the crackling fire and listened to the whistling wind that rattled the windows. "I want to find the construction date and who purchased or built the house. I haven't been able to find anything back far enough. Mostly just social columns and news about other places in town."

Mom stood up and put more wood in the fireplace. "Where have you looked so far?"

Author Biography

Marjorie is the author of Bess's Magical Garden, a middle grade novel and picture book Gramma Mouse Tells a Story. Marjorie is a member of the Society of Children's Book Writers and Illustrators, Writer's Guild of Alberta and Rave Reviews Book Club. Her short story The Ghost of Rose Cottage is published in Ghostly Writes Anthology 2016 published by Plaisted Publishing House. Other work has been published in Channillo series, titled Ghostly Encounter and other short stories, this is listed in the short story section. https://www.channillo.com

Marjorie has been an avid reader since early childhood and has always been imaginative. Growing up on a farm before television aided in her using her imagination to create a variety of pastimes. Stories formed in her mind but most of them were never written down until later in life. It wasn't until her children were growing up that she started to take art and writing courses. At that time, her writing improved and short stories formed. It was when she retired that the idea for Bess's Magical Garden surfaced.

After Marjorie's divorce she worked in the plant industry. First at a greenhouse and then looking after tropical plants in downtown offices. For awhile it looked like her adult children would never leave home but they have now all flown the nest and are having their own life's adventures. After retirement she moved to Strathmore where she lives with her pets.

Website: https://mhembroff.wordpress.com
www.amazon.com/author/mehembroff
https://www.facebook.com/mehembroff
https://twitter.com/margiesart1
http://www.goodreads.com/mehembroff

Thank you to my Readers

Thank you for reading my book and it would mean a great deal to me if you could give me your opinion. Not only will this let me know what you feel about my writing in general, but potential readers will also value your feedback.

Reviews can be left on
http://www.amazon.com
https://www.goodreads.com

If you purchased your book on Amazon, you already have an account. Just state whether you purchased or received the book as a gift. If you don't feel comfortable leaving your name create a pen name which will protect your privacy. There are thousands of books listed in Goodreads and this is a good way of finding books in your favorite genre. It is easy to get an account as a reader.

Finally, I would be delighted to hear from you by email mehembroff@hotmail.ca or margiesart@hotmail.com about the book.

Here are some tips to help you create your review
1.   Who is your favorite character?
2.   Who is your least favorite character?
3.   What did you like the best in the story?
4.   Did you like the cover and how the book was laid out inside? Was it easy to read?
5.   Would you recommend the book to others?

Thank you very much for taking the time to let me know your opinion. Best wishes Marjorie Hembroff.

Made in the USA
Columbia, SC
29 August 2018